"Everything will be all right, Jo," Dekker had said.

And Dekker was not the kind of man to offer empty promises. If he said things would be all right, they would be. So Joleen just knew that her best friend had found a way out of this tight spot she'd gotten herself into. But how?

"Dekker," she said, "I appreciate your offering to help, but I can't allow you to spend money you don't have to help me keep little Sam."

"Jo, I'm a rich man now. A millionaire."

"I...I..."

"You're sputtering." He chuckled.

He was grinning, and she peered at him suspiciously. "There's more?"

"You bet. There's my solution to your problem of a custody fight over Sam. It came to me like a bolt from the blue." He paused.

"Dekker. What?" she demanded. *"What?"*

"Marry me, Jo."

Dear Reader,

"It was a high like no other," says Elaine Nichols. She's speaking, of course, about getting "the call." After numerous submissions, Elaine sold her first manuscript to Silhouette Special Edition and we're pleased to publish *Cowgirl Be Mine* this month—a reunion romance between a heroine whose body needs healing and a hero whose wounds are hidden inside. Elaine has many more Special Edition books planned, so keep an eye out for this fresh new voice.

And be sure to pick up all the novels Special Edition has to offer. Marrying the Bravo fortune heir granted the heroine custody of her son, but once the two are under the same roof, they're *unable* to sleep in separate beds, in Christine Rimmer's *The Marriage Conspiracy*. Then a hungry reporter wishes his tempting waitress would offer him a tasty dish of *her* each morning, in *Dateline Matrimony* by reader favorite Gina Wilkins.

What's *The Truth About Tate?* Marilyn Pappano tells you when her journalist heroine threatens to expose the illegitimate brother of the hero, a man who would do anything to protect his family. She hadn't giggled since her mother died, so *His Little Girl's Laughter* by Karen Rose Smith is music to Rafe Pierson's ears. And in Tori Carrington's *The Woman for Dusty Conrad,* a firefighter hero has returned to divorce his wife, but discovers a still-burning flame.

We hope you enjoy this month's exciting selections, and if you have a dream of being published, like Elaine Nichols, please send a self-addressed stamped query letter to my attention at: Silhouette Books, 300 East 42nd St, 6th floor, New York, NY 10017.

Best,

Karen Taylor Richman
Senior Editor

Please address questions and book requests to:
Silhouette Reader Service
U.S.: 3010 Walden Ave., P.O. Box 1325, Buffalo, NY 14269
Canadian: P.O. Box 609, Fort Erie, Ont. L2A 5X3

Christine Rimmer

THE MARRIAGE CONSPIRACY

Silhouette®

SPECIAL EDITION™

Published by Silhouette Books

America's Publisher of Contemporary Romance

For those who sought friendship
and found lasting love…

 SILHOUETTE BOOKS

ISBN 0-373-24423-1

THE MARRIAGE CONSPIRACY

Copyright © 2001 by Christine Rimmer

This edition published by arrangement with Harlequin Books S.A.

® and TM are trademarks of Harlequin Books S.A., used under license. Trademarks indicated with ® are registered in the United States Patent and Trademark Office, the Canadian Trade Marks Office and in other countries.

Visit Silhouette at www.eHarlequin.com

Printed in U.S.A.

Books by Christine Rimmer

CHRISTINE RIMMER

came to her profession the long way around. Before settling down to write about the magic of romance, she'd been an actress, a salesclerk, a janitor, a model, a phone sales representative, a teacher, a waitress, a playwright and an office manager. She insists she never had a problem keeping a job—she was merely gaining "life experience" for her future as a novelist. Christine is grateful not only for the joy she finds in writing, but for what waits when the day's work is through: a man she loves, who loves her right back, and the privilege of watching their children grow and change day to day. She lives with her family in Oklahoma.

THE BRAVOS

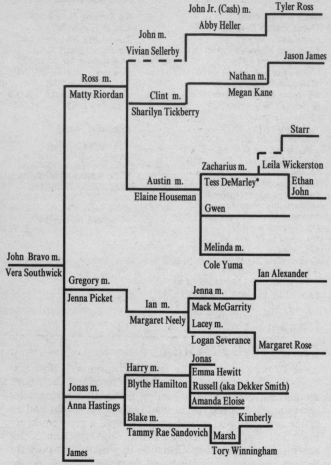

John Jr. (Cash) m. Tyler Ross
Abby Heller

John m.
Vivian Sellerby

Jason James

Nathan m.
Megan Kane

Ross m.
Matty Riordan

Clint m.
Sharilyn Tickberry

Starr

Zacharius m. Leila Wickerston
Tess DeMarley*

Ethan
John

Austin m.
Elaine Houseman

Gwen

Melinda m.
Cole Yuma

John Bravo m.
Vera Southwick

Ian Alexander

Gregory m.
Jenna Picket

Jenna m.
Mack McGarrity

Ian m.
Margaret Neely

Lacey m.
Logan Severance Margaret Rose

Jonas
Emma Hewitt

Harry m.
Blythe Hamilton

Russell (aka Dekker Smith)

Amanda Eloise

Jonas m.
Anna Hastings

Kimberly

Blake m.
Tammy Rae Sandovich Marsh

Tory Winningham

James

(Broken lines indicate previous marriages)
*One child from a previous marriage: Jobeth

Chapter One

It was hot, without a hint of a breeze. Mid-October and it felt like the dog days of August. The wedding guests wandered beneath the sweet gums and pecan trees that shaded Camilla Tilly's backyard, faces shining with sweat, sipping cold drinks in which the ice melted too soon.

Joleen Tilly, Camilla's oldest daughter and sister to the bride, stood at the cake table from which she'd just shooed away three frosting-licking children. Joleen felt as if *she* was melting in her ankle-length rose-colored satin and lace bridesmaid's gown.

And she couldn't help suspecting that the cake was melting, too. The icing looked thinner, didn't it, in a couple of places? The cake had five layers, each bordered with icing swags and accented with buttercream roses. Hadn't the top four layers slid sideways the tiniest bit, wasn't the whole thing leaning to the right, just a little?

Joleen shook her head—at the cake, at her own discomfort, at the whole situation. She had tried to convince her sister to rent a hall, but DeDe dug in her heels and announced that she'd always dreamed of getting married in Mama's backyard. There was no budging DeDe once she dug in her heels.

So here they all were. Melting.

And way behind schedule. The ceremony was supposed to have started an hour ago. But Dekker Smith, the closest thing the Tilly sisters had to a big brother and the one who had promised to give DeDe away, had yet to arrive.

As Joleen stewed about the missing Dekker, about the cake, about the sweltering heat, her uncle Hubert Tilly wandered over, beer in hand. He stood beside her, leaned her way and spoke out of the corner of his mouth. "It's about time we got this thing started, don't you think?"

"Yes. And we will, Uncle Hubert. Real soon."

"Good." Her uncle lifted his beer to her in a toast. "Here's to you, Joly. We all know it's bound to be your turn next." He threw back his big head and drank.

Joleen, who sometimes got a little tired of hearing how it would be "her turn next," smiled resolutely and watched uncle Hubert's Adam's apple bounce up and down as he drained the can.

"Well, what do you know?" Uncle Hubert said when he was through guzzling. "It's empty." The can made groaning, cracking sounds as he crushed it in his beefy fist. "Better get another..." He headed off toward the coolers lined up against the garden shed. Joleen watched him go, hoping he wouldn't get too drunk before the day was over.

She turned her attention to the cake again and decided that it should not sit out here in this heat for one minute longer. Her mother's Colonial Revival house had been built in 1923. But thirty years ago, when her father bought it, one of the first things he'd done to it was to put in central heat and air.

She grabbed herself a couple of big, strong cousins—a Tilly, from her father's side and a DuFrayne, from her mother's. "Pick up that cake table," she told them. "And do it carefully."

The cousins lifted the table.

"Okay, good. This way…" Joleen backed toward the kitchen door slowly, patting the air with outstretched hands and speaking to her cousins in soothing tones. "Watch it…careful…that's right…." She opened the door for them and ushered them into the coolness of her mother's kitchen. "Watch that step. Easy. Good."

Once she'd closed the door behind them, she led them to the little section of wall on the far side of the breakfast nook. "Right here, out of the way. Just set it down easy." The cousins put the table down.

Joleen let out a long, relieved sigh. "Perfect. Thank you, boys."

"No problem," said Burly, the DuFrayne cousin. His full name was Wilbur, but everyone had always called him Burly. "When's this thing getting started, anyway?"

"Soon, real soon," Joleen promised, thinking about

Dekker again with a tightening in her tummy that was a little bit from irritation and a lot from worry.

Dekker had called yesterday afternoon and left a message on the machine at Joleen's house. He said he wouldn't make it for the rehearsal, after all, but that he'd be there in plenty of time for the wedding. Joleen wished she'd been home when he called. She would have gotten some specifics out of him—like a flight number and an arrival time, for starters.

And maybe even an idea of what the heck this particular trip was about, anyway. Dekker had told her nothing so far. The last time she'd actually spoken to him, early last Wednesday morning, he would only say that he was leaving for Los Angeles right away. He'd promised he'd be back in time for the rehearsal— which, as it turned out, he was not.

Joleen assumed it must be a business trip. A lot of his clients insisted on strict confidentiality, so that would account for his being so hush-hush about the whole thing. And sometimes, she knew, his job could be dangerous. Was this one of those times?

Joleen pushed that scary thought right out of her mind.

She'd tried more than once to reach him on his mobile phone. And each time she did, she got a recorded voice telling her that the "customer" wasn't available and offering her the chance to leave her name and number. She *had* left her name and number. But she'd never heard back.

"Joly, you are lookin' strained," said the Tilly cousin, whose name was Bud. "You okay?"

"Well, of course I am." She arranged her face into what she hoped resembled a confident smile. "Help yourselves to a beer. There's plenty. Outside in the coolers. And right there in the fridge, too.''

Bud and Burly turned for the refrigerator. Joleen went out the kitchen door again, into the blistering backyard.

Her aunt LeeAnne DuFrayne, Burly's mama, was standing under one of the two patio ceiling fans, holding the front of her dress out at the neck so that the fan's breeze could cool her a little. As Joleen went by, Aunt LeeAnne let go of her dress and caught Joleen's arm.

''You have done a beautiful job here, hon.''

''You're a sweetheart to say so, Aunt LeeAnne. Too bad it's so darn hot.''

''You can't control the weather, hon.''

''I know, I know.''

''The backyard looks festive. And Mesta Park is such a lovely area. I always admire it so every time I visit.''

Mesta Park lay in the heart of Oklahoma City, a charming old neighborhood with lots of classic prairie-style houses and graceful mature trees. Joleen's mother had owned the house on Northwest Seventeenth Street since she herself had been a young bride.

Aunt LeeAnne patted Joleen's arm. ''I do think we ought to start the ceremony soon, though, don't you?''

''Soon,'' Joleen repeated. What else could she say?

Aunt LeeAnne stopped patting. She gripped Joleen's arm and whispered in her ear, ''I see that you invited the Atwoods.''

Joleen made a noise in the affirmative and flicked a quick glance toward the well-dressed couple standing by themselves near the punch table. Bobby Atwood, the couple's only son, had died just six weeks ago, in a power-skiing accident on Lake Thunderbird. Pictures of the funeral service had dominated the local news. Atwood, after all, was an important name in the state of Oklahoma.

In spite of what had happened between herself and Bobby, the sight of his grieving parents at graveside had proved too much for Joleen. She hadn't been able to stop herself from reaching out to them.

"You have a good heart, Joly," whispered Aunt LeeAnne. "There aren't many who would be so forgiving."

"Well, it seemed like a nice gesture, to ask them if they'd like to come."

Aunt LeeAnne made a small, sympathetic noise and patted Joleen's arm some more.

Joleen added, "And I do want Sam to know his father's parents."

Sam. Just the thought of her little boy lightened Joleen's mood. She looked for him, caught sight of him with her younger sister, thirteen-year-old Niki, about twenty feet away, near the tall white picket fence that surrounded her mother's backyard on three sides. Niki, in a rose-red dress identical to Joleen's, had agreed to watch Sam so that Joleen could handle all the details of running the wedding.

Sam had his daddy's hair, thick and straight and sandy colored. As Joleen watched, he threw back that sandy head and let out his almost-a-baby laugh. At the sound of that laugh, Joleen's heart seemed to get bigger inside her chest.

Then she noticed that Bobby's father was staring right at her.

Robert Atwood quickly looked away. But not before she saw a lot more than she wanted to see in his cold, gray glance. Her little boy's grandfather did not approve of her. And he was looking down his snooty nose at the members of her family.

The Atwoods moved in the best circles. They hung out with the governor and his pretty wife, attended all the most important political and social events in the city. Robert Atwood's expression made it painfully clear that he found this small-scale backyard wedding to be tacky and totally beneath him.

And now he was staring at Sam. So was his wife, Antonia. The woman wore a look of longing so powerful it sent a chill down Joleen's spine in spite of the heat.

I probably should have listened to Dekker, Joleen thought. Dekker—who'd better show up soon or they were going ahead without him—had warned her to stay away from Robert Atwood and his wife.

"Unless you're after a little of the Atwood money," he'd said. "Sam *is* entitled to some of that."

"It is not the money, Dekker. Honestly. We're gettin' by all right."

"Okay. Then forget the Atwoods. They have too much money and too much power and, given the kind of son they raised, I'd say they're way too likely to abuse both."

She had punched him playfully on the arm. "You are so cynical it scares me sometimes."

"You ought to be scared of the Atwoods, of the trouble they'll probably cause you if you tell them about Sam. I mean it. Take my advice and stay away from them."

But she hadn't taken her friend's advice. Robert Atwood sold real estate on a grand scale. He dealt in shopping centers and medical complexes and skyscrapers with a thousand and one offices in them. She had called him at Atwood and Son Property Development.

At first, Bobby's father had refused to see her or to believe that his precious son could have fathered a child he didn't even know about. In the end, though, the hope that there might be something of Bobby left on the earth must have been too powerful to deny. He had called Joleen and asked if he and his wife might meet Sam. And as soon as they set eyes on her baby boy, they knew who his father had to be.

"Joly, hon…"

Joleen looked into her aunt's flushed face and smiled. "Hmm?"

"I just have to say this. I have got a powerful feeling that we will be watching you take your walk down the aisle very soon now." Aunt LeeAnne beamed up at her.

Joleen kept her smile. But it did get old sometimes.

Here's to you, Joly. We all know it's bound to be your turn next….

I just know you are going to meet someone so special….

I see a man in your future, hon. The right man this time….

Those she loved would not stop telling her that true love and happily-ever-after were coming her way.

Joleen fully understood why they did it. None of them could quite believe that she, the levelheaded one, the both-feet-firmly-on-the-ground one, had gone and fallen for a rich boy's honeyed lies.

They felt sorry for her. They wanted the best for her.

And to them the best meant a good man to stand at her side, a husband to help her raise her child.

"I don't think so, Aunt LeeAnne."

"Well, you just think what you want. I am right about this and you will see that I am."

Oh, please, Joleen thought. As if she even had *time* for love and romance at this point in her life. She had a toddler to raise and a business to run—not to mention a recently delinquent thirteen-year-old sister and a stunningly beautiful fifty-year-old widowed mother who somehow managed to fall in and out of love on what seemed like a weekly basis. DeDe might be off her hands after today, but Niki and her mother still counted on Joleen to be there whenever they needed her.

And really, Joleen didn't mind being the one they counted on. She was happy. She honestly was. With her precious little son and her beloved if somewhat troublesome mama and sisters, with the beauty salon she and her mother operated together and with lots of loving family and good friends—including Dekker, who in the past few years had become her closest friend.

Dekker, who was now so late she doubted he would make it at all.

Nope. It would not be Joleen's turn next. Not for a decade or so, at least. Maybe more than a decade. Maybe never. In any case, not "next."

But she didn't tell her aunt LeeAnne that. Instead,

she hooked her arm around her aunt's round shoulders and gave a loving squeeze. "Whatever you say."

By three-thirty, Joleen decided they had waited long enough. She left the drooping guests behind beneath the pecan trees, entered the house and climbed the stairs to her mother's big bedroom on the second floor, which today was serving as the bride's dressing room.

DeDe, who looked absolutely breathtaking in floor-length white satin, came at her the minute Joleen appeared in the doorway. "Where is he? Is he here yet?"

Joleen shook her head.

"Oh, no." DeDe stopped in midstride and caught her full lower lip between her small white teeth. "How's Wayne holdin' up?"

Wayne Thornton was DeDe's groom. "Wayne is great. He's down in the kitchen right now, hanging out with Bud and Burly."

"He's not mad?"

"Wayne? Are you kidding?" Wayne Thornton was a veterinarian. He was also about the calmest, most easygoing person Joleen had ever had the pleasure to meet. "I promise you, Wayne is fine. Waiting patiently, swapping jokes with Bud and Burly."

"I want to see him."

"Well, all right, I'll just—"

"Wait. Stop right there."

Joleen did as her sister commanded.

"What do you think you're doing?" DeDe accused. "You know I can't see him. It would be bad luck."

Joleen lifted a shoulder in the tiniest of shrugs. Of course, she knew that. But if she'd been the one to say it, her sister would have insisted that Joleen run

downstairs that instant and come right back up with
Wayne. Like Niki, DeDe had had some troubled times
in the past. She'd settled down a lot in the last couple
of years, but she hadn't gotten rid of her stubborn
streak, of a certain contrariness to her nature. Joleen
never locked horns with her if she could avoid it.
Locking horns with DeDe almost never paid off.

DeDe sighed. "I'm goin' nuts." She whirled in a
rustle of satin, flounced to their mother's big four-
poster bed, turned and plunked herself down on the
edge of it. "Where *is* Dekker?"

Joleen approached and sat beside her sister. She
took DeDe's hand. "Honey..."

DeDe yanked her hand away. "Don't say it. He
promised he would be here and we are gonna wait for
him."

"Honey, we *have* waited. For over an hour. You
have to think of your guests. They are dyin' out
there."

"Well, I can't help it. It wouldn't be right to start
without Dekker. You know that it wouldn't."

Joleen had no quick comeback for that.

The problem was, in her heart, Joleen *agreed* with
DeDe. It *wouldn't* be right to start without Dekker.

Dekker Smith might not be blood to them, but he
truly was family. His mama, Lorraine, had been *their*
mama's best friend. Lorraine was gone now, and Dekker hadn't lived next door since he graduated high
school, but he looked out for them all, especially in
the past ten years, since Joleen's father had died.

Dekker spent his holidays with them. He had been
the one who taught both Joleen and DeDe how to
drive. He could always be counted upon to show up

with his toolbox when something needed fixing—not to mention to stand up for any female named Tilly any time things got rough. Two years ago, when DeDe had her little run-in with the law, Dekker had gone with Joleen to the police station to bail her out and he'd made sure she got the best lawyer around. Same thing with Niki, when she'd been in trouble last year. Dekker was right there, to help out.

He was family in the deepest way, and of course DeDe wanted him there to see her married.

But they couldn't wait all day to start the wedding march. "DeDe, I think we are just going to have to go ahead."

"But we *can't* go ahead," DeDe cried.

"Yes, we can. And you know that Dekker will understand. You know that he—"

"*I* won't understand. Don't you get it? I want Dekker to give me away."

"Well, I know you do, but he is not here."

DeDe glared. "Oh, you, Joly. Always so *logical*. I cannot stand to hear logic at a time like this."

"Well, I am so sorry to be reasonable when you would rather not, but—"

DeDe cut her off by bursting into tears.

Joleen closed her eyes and silently counted to ten.

When she opened them again, she saw her mother, Camilla, hovering in the doorway to the hall. "What is it, baby? What has happened here?"

"Joly says we have to go ahead." DeDe sobbed. "She says we can't wait for Dekker."

"Oh, now, honey…"

"I want him here, Mama. I want him to give me away."

"Yes, and we all understand that."

"It won't seem right if he isn't here."

"Oh, I know, I know…"

DeDe let out a frustrated wail. The cry brought Camilla out of the doorway. She rushed across the room, slender arms outstretched. Joleen slid to the side and got out of the way. DeDe stood. Camilla gathered her close.

"Aw, baby," Camilla cooed. "Now, you know you are going to ruin your face, carrying on like this. Now, you just settle down…."

But DeDe was not settling down.

And Camilla had started crying, too. Tears filled her huge brown eyes and spilled down her cheeks. Sobs constricted her long white throat. Joleen backed away a few more steps, as her middle sister and her mother held on to each other and wailed.

"Honey, honey," Camilla cried. "Don't you worry. It's okay. We will wait. We will wait until Dekker gets here. We'll wait forever, if we have to. Till the end of time, I swear it to you…."

There was a gasp from the doorway. Joleen looked over.

Niki. She had Sam perched on her hip—and her hazel eyes were already brimming. Sam had a teething biscuit stuck in his mouth. He sucked it steadily, not much disturbed by all the excitement on the other side of the room.

But then, why should he be disturbed? His grandmother and his aunts never hid their emotions. He was used to lots of crying and carrying on.

"Mama?" Niki gulped back a sob. "DeDe? What is going on?"

Her mother and middle sister only cried all the harder. Niki's face started to crumple.

Joleen reached Niki's side in three quick steps. "Before you start," she warned, "give me my baby."

"Here." Niki held Sam out. He reached for Joleen automatically, gurgling, "Mama!" And then his biscuit-gooey little hands encircled her neck, his soft weight was on her arm and his sweet, slightly dusty smell filled her senses.

With a hard sob, Niki flew across the room. Camilla and DeDe enfolded her into their embrace. The three hugged and bawled, their arms around each other, a sniffling, tear-streaked huddle of satin and lace.

Joleen stood a few feet from the door, resolutely calm as always, holding her baby and watching her mother and sisters wail and moan, wondering how in the world she would manage to calm them all now.

"What is this, a wedding—or a wake?"

Joleen turned toward the sound of that deep, wry voice. It was Dekker, in the doorway. He had made it, after all.

Chapter Two

Relief washed through Joleen—and a sweet rush of affection, as well. She should probably be good and angry with him for being so late, but how could she be angry when she was so glad to see him? And he looked so handsome in the nice lightweight suit they had picked out together just for this occasion.

He also looked...easy within himself and relaxed. Something good must have happened out there in Los Angeles.

"You're late," she muttered.

He shrugged. "Air travel is not what it used to be. I sat at O'Hare for ten hours."

"Your cell phone—"

"Needs recharging. Sorry. I tried to call you."

"At my house?"

"Right. From a pay phone, this morning around eight."

"I left at seven-thirty."

"And I also called here. Twice. Got a busy signal both times."

She wasn't surprised. The house had been full of people all day and the phone had been in constant use.

"Dek!" Sam shouted. He let go of Joleen's neck and reached for the man in the doorway.

"Whoa, big guy." Dekker stepped up and took him.

About then, DeDe stopped sobbing long enough to glance across the room. "Dekker! You made it!"

The three Tilly women broke from their huddle and rushed for the door. Joleen got out of their way again. They surrounded Dekker and Sam, all of them talking at once.

"Where *were* you?"

"We've been waiting for *hours*...."

"We were so afraid you wouldn't make it."

"Is everything all right?"

"Is everything—"

He chuckled. "Everything's fine. There was just a little matter of a long delay between flights. But I am here now." He had Sam on one arm. He wrapped the other around DeDe, who looked up at him through shining eyes. "And I am ready to give away this gorgeous bride."

Twenty minutes later, down in the backyard beneath the pecan trees, the wedding march began. A blessed breeze had actually come up, so it wasn't quite as stifling as it had been for most of the day. The ceremony went off without a hitch. And when Wayne Thornton kissed his bride, everyone could see that this was a true, love match.

Joleen had had her reservations, when DeDe and Wayne first announced that they would marry. After all, DeDe *was* only twenty. It seemed young to Joleen.

But looking at the two of them as they repeated their vows, Joleen let go of her doubts. Wayne was a good, steady man. And DeDe adored him almost as much as he worshipped her. In the end, Joleen supposed, the two had as good a chance as any couple at lasting a lifetime side by side.

She was pouring more ginger ale into the punch bowl, feeling kind of misty-eyed and contented for the first time that day, when Dekker appeared at her side.

"What the hell are the Atwoods doing here?" He spoke low, for her ears alone.

She gave him her most determined smile and whispered back, "I invited them."

"Damn it, Jo. I hope you know what you're doing."

"Me, too—and would you go in and get me some more of this ginger ale?"

Midnight-blue eyes regarded her steadily. "I wish you had listened to me."

"I did listen—then I did what I thought was right." She waved the empty bottle at him. "Ginger ale? Please?"

Shaking his head, he turned for the back door.

The afternoon wore on.

Camilla, on something of an emotional roller coaster this special day when her middle baby was getting married, had a little too much sparkling wine and flirted blatantly with anyone willing to flirt back.

"You probably ought to say something to her, hon," advised Aunt LeeAnne as Joleen was putting the finishing touches on the buffet.

Joleen shook her head and took the lid off a chafing dish. "My mother is a flirt. Always has been, always will be. I have enough to worry about without trying to fight a person's nature."

"When your father was still with us—"

"I know. All her flirting was for him then. She never looked at another man. But he's been gone for so long now. And she is still very much alive. She will never stop lookin' for the kind of love she had once."

"So sad…" Aunt LeeAnne looked mournful.

Camilla's musical laughter rang out as she pulled one of the groom's uncles from a chair and made him dance with her.

"I don't know," said Joleen. "Seems to me that she's having a pretty good time."

Aunt LeeAnne picked up a toothpick and speared a meatball from the chafing dish. "Mmm. Delicious. What is that spice?"

"Cumin?"

"Could be—or maybe curry?"

"No. I don't think there's any curry in those meatballs."

Aunt LeeAnne helped herself to a second meatball, then shrugged. "Well, I suppose you're right about Camilla…."

Uncle Hubert Tilly staggered by, yet another beer clutched in his fist.

Aunt LeeAnne clucked her tongue. "Now, there is someone to worry about. He has been drinkin' all afternoon, and in this heat…" Aunt LeeAnne frowned. "He looks peaked, don't you think?"

"True," said Joleen. "He does not look well."

"Someone really should talk to him…." Aunt

LeeAnne gazed at Joleen hopefully. Joleen refused to take the hint, so her aunt added with clear reluctance, "Someone of his own generation, I suppose."

"Be my guest."

So Aunt LeeAnne DuFrayne trotted off to try to convince Uncle Hubert Tilly that he'd had enough beer.

Uncle Hubert didn't take the news well. "What?" he shouted, leaning against the trunk of the sweet gum in the southwest corner of the yard. "I've had enough? What're you talkin' about, LeeAnne? There ain' no such thing as enough."

Aunt LeeAnne tried to whisper something into his ear. He shrugged her off and stumbled away. Aunt LeeAnne pinched up her mouth for a minute, then shook her head and returned to the buffet table.

"Well, I guess you are right, Joly. There is no savin' that man from himself."

"You tried your best." Joleen handed her aunt a plate. "Taste those buffalo wings. And the pasta primavera is pretty good, too."

Aunt LeeAnne took the plate and began to load it with food.

Out of the corner of her eye, Joleen could see Robert Atwood, standing at the edge of the patio, Antonia, as always, close at his side. Robert wore a look of aloof disdain on his distinguished face as he watched Uncle Hubert's unsteady progress toward the coolers lined up by the garden shed.

"Joly, is that pickled okra I see?"

Joleen turned her widest smile on another of her father's brothers. "You bet it is, Uncle Stan. Help yourself."

"I surely will."

With the buffet all ready to go, Joleen went to check on the punch table again. The bowl needed filling. She took care of that. Then she went back inside to look for those little frilly toothpicks that everyone kept using up the minute she set them out.

She got stalled in the kitchen for several minutes. Burly had a traveling-salesman joke she just had to hear. Once he'd told it and she had finished laughing, she found the toothpicks and headed for the back door once more.

Outside again, she discovered that her mother was dancing with yet another of the guests from Wayne's family. And Aunt LeeAnne whispered in her ear that Uncle Hubert had gone behind the garden shed to be sick.

Joleen suppressed a sigh. "I'll go see to him."

"I think that would be best. I'd do it, of course, but you saw what happened the last time I tried to give the poor man a hand."

When Joleen got to the other side of the shed, she spotted two little DuFraynes and a small niece of Wayne's peeking around the far end. Uncle Hubert sagged pitifully against the shed wall, his head stuck in among the dark pink blooms of a tall crape myrtle bush.

She dealt with the children first. "You kids go on now."

The three stared for a moment, then began giggling.

"I mean it. Do not make me get your mamas."

The giggling stopped. Three sets of wide eyes regarded her. Joleen put on a no-nonsense glare and made a sharp shooing gesture with the back of her hand.

The three vanished around the end of the shed, giggles erupting again as soon as they were out of sight. The giggles faded away.

Uncle Hubert groaned. And then his thick shoulders shook. Joleen swallowed and pressed her lips together as she heard splattering sounds behind the bush.

She waited until that attack of sickness had passed. Then she dared to move a few steps closer. "Uncle Hubert…"

Her uncle groaned. "Joly?"

"That's right."

"Go 'way." He spoke into the crape myrtle bush.

Joleen edged a little closer. "Uncle Hubert, I want you to come in the house with me now."

"I'm fine." He groaned again. "Go 'way."

"No. No, you listen. It's too hot out here. You can lie down inside."

"No." He made a strangled sound. His shoulders shook again, but this time nothing seemed to be coming up.

Joleen waited, to make sure he was finished. Then, with slow care, she moved right up next to him. "Come on, now…" She laid a hand on his arm. "You just come on."

"No!' He jerked away, half stumbling, almost falling, bouncing with a muffled gonging sound against the metal wall of the garden shed. "Leave," he growled. "Go…"

Joleen stepped back again, unwilling to give up but unsure how to convince him that he should come with her.

A hand clasped her shoulder.

Dekker. She knew it before she even turned to see him standing right behind her. She felt easier instantly. Between them they would manage. They always did.

"Need help?"

She nodded.

He raised a dark brow. "You want him in the house?"

She nodded again.

He stepped around her. "Hubert..."

"Ugh. Wha? Oh. Dek."

"Right. Come on, man. Let's go..."

"Ugh..."

"Yeah. You need to stretch out."

"Uh-uh..."

Dekker took Uncle Hubert's arm and wrapped it across his broad shoulder. Uncle Hubert moaned. He kept saying no and shaking his head. But he didn't pull away. Slowly Dekker turned him around and got him moving.

Joleen went on ahead, warning the other guests out of the way, opening the back door, leading the way through the kitchen and into the hall. Uncle Hubert would probably be most comfortable upstairs in one of the bedrooms, but she didn't know how far he'd be willing to let Dekker drag him. So she settled for the living room.

"Here," she said, "on the couch." She tossed away her mother's favorite decorative pillows as she spoke, then spread an old afghan across the cushions. It would provide some protection if Uncle Hubert's poor stomach decided to rebel again.

Dekker eased the other man down. Uncle Hubert fell onto his back with a long, low groan.

"Let's get his shoes off," said Dekker, already kneeling at Uncle Hubert's feet. Before he had the second shoe off, Uncle Hubert was snoring. Dekker set the shoes, side by side, beneath the coffee table. "They'll be right here whenever he needs them."

Joleen stood over her uncle, shaking her head. "It seems like we ought to *do* something, doesn't it? We shouldn't let him go on hurting himself this way."

Uncle Hubert had lost his wife, Thelma, six months ago. The heavy beer drinking had started not long after that.

"Give him time," Dekker said. "He'll work it out."

"I hope he works it out soon. A man's liver can only take so much."

"He will," Dekker said. "He'll get through it."

They were good words to hear, especially from Dekker, who had never been the most optimistic guy on the block. "You sound so certain."

He winked at her. "I oughtta know, don't you think?"

They shared a long look, one full of words they didn't really need to say out loud.

Three years ago, Dekker's wife, Stacey, had died. His mama, Lorraine, had passed away not long after. Dekker had done quite a bit of drinking himself in the months following those two sad events.

Dekker said, "Maybe you ought to start whipping up a few casseroles."

It was a joke between them now, how Joleen had kept after him, dropping in at his place several times a week, pouring his booze down the drain and urging him to "talk out his pain."

He wouldn't talk. But she wouldn't give up on him, either. She brought him casseroles to make sure he ate right and kept dragging him out to go bowling and to the movies. Good, nourishing food and a few social activities *had* made a difference.

It had also brought them closer. She was, after all, five years younger than Dekker. Five years, while they were growing up, had seemed like a lifetime. Almost as if they were of different generations.

But it didn't seem that way anymore. Now they were equals.

They were best friends.

She said, "You still have not bothered to tell me why you thought you had to fly off to Los Angeles out of nowhere like that."

"Later," he said. "There's a lot to tell and now is not the time."

"Were you…in danger?"

"No."

"Was it something for a client?"

"Jo. Please. Not now."

On the couch, Hubert stiffened, snorted and then went on snoring even louder than before.

Dekker said, "I think we've done all we can for him at the moment."

"Guess so. Might as well get back to the party. We're probably out of frilly toothpicks again."

Dekker grinned. "DeDe grabbed me a few minutes ago. Something about cutting the cake?"

"No. It's too early. They're still attacking the buffet

table. But it is a little cooler now. Safe to get everything set up.''

''Safe?''

''That's right. We can chance taking the cake back outside.''

''This sounds ominous.''

''A wedding can be a scary time.''

''Tell me about it.''

She took his big, blunt-fingered hand. ''Come on.''

They left Uncle Hubert snoring on the couch and went out to the kitchen, where they enlisted Burly to help Dekker carry the cake back out to the patio.

Once the cake was in position for cutting, Joleen went looking for Niki and Sam. She found them on the front porch, building a castle out of Duplo blocks.

''Mama. Look.'' Sam beamed her his biggest, proudest smile.

''Wonderful job, baby.'' She asked Niki, ''Did he eat anything yet?''

Niki nodded. ''He had some corn. And that fruit dish—the one with the coconut? Oh, and he ate about five of those little meatballs.''

''Milk?''

''Yeah—and what's with those Atwood people?''

What do you mean? Joleen wanted to demand. *What did they do?*

She held the questions back. Sam might be only eighteen months old, but you could never be sure of how much he understood. And she didn't want Niki stirred up, either. She gestured with a toss of her head. Niki got up and followed her down to the other end of the long porch.

"What do you mean about the Atwoods?" Joleen kept her voice low and her tone even.

Niki shrugged. "I don't know. They sure stare a lot."

"Have they...bothered you?"

"I don't know, Joly. Like I said, they just stare."

"They haven't spoken to you at all?"

"Well, yeah. Twice. They tried to talk to Sam, but you know how he is sometimes. He got shy, buried his head against my shoulder. Both times they gave up and walked away."

So. They had tried to get to know their grandson a little and gotten nowhere. Joleen found herself feeling sorry for them again.

"No real problems, though?"

"Uh-uh. Just general creepiness."

Joleen reached out, brushed a palm along her sister's arm. "You've been great, taking care of Sam all day."

"Yeah. Call me Wonder Girl." Niki was good with Sam. She took her baby-sitting duties seriously. In fact, Niki was doing a lot better lately all the way around. She'd given them a real scare last year. But Joleen had begun to believe those problems were behind her now.

"Want a little break?"

"Sure— Can I get out of this dress?"

Joleen hid a smile. Rose-colored satin was hardly her little sister's style. Niki liked black. Black hip-riding bellbottom jeans, skinny little black T-shirts, black Doc Martens. Sometimes, for variety, she'd wear navy blue or deep purple, but never anything bright. Certainly nothing rosy red.

"Go ahead and change," said Joleen.

Niki beamed. "Thanks."

They rejoined Sam at the other end of the porch. "Hey, big guy," Joleen said. "I need some help."

Sam loved to "help." He considered "helping" to be anything that involved a lot of busyness on his part. Pulling his mother around by her thumb could be "helping," or carrying items from one place to another.

Sam set down the red plastic block in his fist and leaned forward, going to his hands and knees. "I hep." He rocked back to the balls of his feet and pushed himself to an upright position.

Joleen held out her arms.

He said something she couldn't really make out, but she knew he meant he wanted to walk.

So she took his hand and walked him down the front steps and around to the backyard. When she spotted the Atwoods alone at a table on the far side of the patio, she led him over there.

Okay, they were snobs. And they made her a little nervous.

But it had to be awkward for them at this party. They didn't really know a soul. Joleen had introduced them to her mother and a few of the guests when they first arrived. But they'd been on their own since then.

All right, maybe Robert Atwood had given her cold looks. Maybe he didn't approve of her. So what?

She was going to get along with them if she could possibly manage it. They were Sammy's grandparents and she would show them respect, give them a little of the slack they didn't appear to be giving her.

And besides, who was to say she hadn't read them

all wrong? Maybe staring and glaring was just Robert Atwood's way of coping with feeling like an outsider.

When she reached their table, Joleen scooped Sam up into her arms. "Well, how are you two holdin' up?"

"We are fine," said Robert.

"Yes," Antonia agreed in that wispy little voice of hers, staring at Sam with misty eyes. "Just fine. Very nice."

Joleen felt a tug of sympathy for the woman. A few weeks ago, when the Atwoods had finally agreed to come to her house and meet Sam, Antonia had shown her one of Bobby's baby pictures. The resemblance to Sam was extraordinary.

What must it be like, to see their lost child every time they looked at Sam?

All the tender goodwill Joleen had felt toward them when she saw the newspaper photos of them at Bobby's funeral came flooding back, filling her with new determination to do all in her power to see that they came to know their only grandson, that they found their rightful place in his life.

"Mind if Sam and I sit down a minute?"

"Please," said Antonia, heartbreakingly eager, grabbing the chair on her right side and pulling it out.

Joleen put Sam in it. He sat back and laid his baby hands on the molded plastic arms. "I sit," he declared with great pride.

Antonia made a small, adoring sound low in her throat.

Joleen took the other free chair at the table. As she scooped her satin skirt smooth beneath her, Robert Atwood spoke again.

"Ahem. Joleen. We really must be leaving soon."

Protestations would have felt a little too phony, so Joleen replied, "Well, I am pleased that you could come and I hope you had a good time."

Robert nodded, his face a cool mask. Antonia seemed too absorbed in watching Sam to make conversation.

Robert said, "I would like a few words with you, before we leave. In private."

That got Antonia's attention. A look of alarm crossed her delicate face. She actually stopped staring at Sam. "Robert, I don't think it's really the time to—"

"I do," her husband interrupted, his voice flat. Final.

Antonia blinked. And said nothing more.

Joleen felt suspicious all over again—not to mention apprehensive. What was the man up to? She honestly wanted to meet these two halfway. But they— Robert, especially—made that so difficult.

She tried to keep her voice light. "Well, if you need to talk to me about something important, today is not the day, I'm afraid. I think I told you, this party is my doing. I'm the one who has to keep things moving along. There's still the cake to cut. And the toasts to be made. Then there will be—"

"I think you could spare us a few minutes, don't you? In the next hour or so?"

"No, I don't think that I—"

"Joleen. It is only a few minutes. I know you can manage it."

Joleen stared into those hard gray eyes. She found herself thinking of Bobby, understanding him a little better, maybe. Even forgiving him some for being so much less than the man she had dreamed him to be. Joleen doubted that Robert Atwood knew how to show love, how to teach a child the true meaning of right and wrong. He would communicate his will—and his sense that he and his were special, above the rules that regular folks had to live by. And his son would grow up as Bobby had. Charming and so handsome. Well dressed, well educated and well mannered. At first glance, a real "catch." A man among men.

But inside, just emptiness. A lack where substance mattered the most.

"Joleen," Bobby had said when she'd told him she was pregnant. "I have zero interest in being a father." The statement had been cool and matter-of-fact, the same kind of tone he might have used to tell her that he didn't feel up to eating Chinese that night. "If you are having a baby, I'm afraid you will be having it on your own."

She'd been so shocked and hurt, she'd reacted on pure pride. "Fine," she had cried. "Get out of my life. I don't want to see you. Ever again."

And Bobby had given her exactly what she'd asked for. He'd walked out of her life—and his unborn child's—and never looked back.

She thought again of Dekker's warnings.

Forget the Atwoods. They have too much money and too much power and given the kind of son they raised, I'd say they're way too likely to abuse both....

She rose from her chair. "Come on, Sam. We've got to get busy here."

Robert Atwood just wouldn't give it up. "A few minutes. Please."

Sam slid off the chair and grabbed her thumb. "We go. I hep." He granted Antonia a shy little smile.

"Joleen," Robert said, making a command out of the sound of her name.

Lord, give me strength, Joleen prayed to her maker. She reminded herself of her original goal here: to develop a reasonably friendly relationship with Sam's daddy's parents. "All right. Let me get through the cutting of the cake. And the toasts. Then we can talk."

"Thank you."

"But only for a few minutes."

"I do understand."

Joleen kept Sam with her, while DeDe and Wayne cut the cake and after, as the guests took turns proposing toasts to the happy couple. Then she handed Sam back to her sister, who was now clad comfortably in her favorite black jeans.

By then it was a little past seven, and growing dark. The breeze had kept up, and the temperature had dropped about ten degrees. It was the next thing to pleasant now, in the backyard. Joleen went around the side of the house and plugged in the paper lanterns that she and a couple of cousins had spent the day before stringing from tree to tree.

There were "oohs" and "ahhs" and a smattering of applause as the glow of the lanterns lit up the deepening night. Joleen felt a glow of her own inside. She had done a good job for her sister. In spite of more than one near disaster, it was stacking up to be a fine wedding, after all.

Camilla had a decent stereo system in the house. And yesterday, after the lantern stringing, Joleen and her cousins had wired up extra speakers and set them out on the patio. So they had good, clear music for dancing. DeDe and Wayne were already swaying beneath the lanterns, held close in each other's arms. So were Aunt LeeAnne and her husband, Uncle Foley, and a number of other couples as well—including Joleen's mother. Camilla moved gracefully in the embrace of yet another middle-aged admirer.

"You did good, Jo." Dekker had come up beside her.

"Thanks."

"Welcome." He was staring out at the backyard, his eyes on the dancers.

Joleen thought of Los Angeles again, wondered what had happened there. She was just about to make another effort at prying some information out of him when she remembered the Atwoods.

She supposed she'd better go looking for them.

Dekker sensed her shift in mood. "What's the matter?"

"Oh, nothin'. Much. I have to say goodbye to the Atwoods."

His brows had drawn together. "I don't like the way you said that. What's going on?"

Teasingly, she bumped his arm with her elbow. "You are such a suspicious man."

"When it comes to Robert Atwood, you bet I am. I don't trust him."

"I noticed. He wants a few minutes with me before they leave, that's all."

"A few minutes for what?"

"I don't know yet. But I'm sure he's plannin' to tell me. When he gets me alone."

"I don't like it."

"Dekker. Chill."

"'When he gets you alone.' What does that mean?"

"It means I am giving him five minutes. In Daddy's study."

"Why? I can tell by the way you're hugging yourself and sighing that you don't want to do that."

"I want to make it work with them."

"People do not always get what they want."

"Dekker—"

He cut her off. "It's pride, Joleen. You know it is. You're ashamed that you had such bad judgment about Bobby. You want them to be different from him. But Jo, they *raised* him. You have to face that."

"I was a fool with Bobby. This is different."

"No. No, I don't think it is."

"You think I'm still a fool?"

He made a sound low in his throat. "Damn it, Jo…"

She stood on tiptoe and whispered to him. "It is only five minutes. Then they will leave and we can enjoy the rest of the party."

"You are too damn trusting."

She planted a quick kiss on his square jaw. "Gotta go."

He was silent as she walked away from him, but she could feel his disapproval, like a chill wind on the warm night. She shrugged it off.

Dekker had seen way too much in his life. He'd been a detective with the OCPD before Stacey died. He'd quit the department during the tough time that followed. But before that he'd seen too many examples of the terrible things people can do to each other.

Now he worked on his own as a private investigator, which gave him an ongoing opportunity to witness more of man's inhumanity to man. Sometimes he saw trouble coming whether it was on the way or not.

Joleen put on a confident smile. She *was* going to do her best to make things work with the Atwoods. It was her duty, as the mother of their grandchild.

She could stand up just fine under Robert Atwood's cold looks and demanding ways. What could he really *do* to her, after all? She held all the power, when it came to their relationship with Sam.

She would not abuse that power. But she wouldn't let Robert Atwood walk all over her, either.

Joleen found the Atwoods waiting by the back door. They followed her into the kitchen and on to the central hall, where Uncle Hubert's snoring could be clearly heard through the open door to the living room.

Joleen held up a hand. ''Just one minute.''

The Atwoods stopped where they were, at the foot of the stairs. Joleen moved to the living room doorway. Uncle Herbert lay just as she and Dekker had left him two hours before, faceup on the couch, his stocking feet dangling a few inches from the floor. Gently she closed the door.

''This way.'' She led Sam's grandparents across the hall to the room her father had used as his study. She reached in and flicked the wall switch. Four tulip-shaped lamps in the small chandelier overhead bloomed into light.

The room was as it had always been. Samuel Tilly's scarred oak desk with its gray swivel chair waited in front of the window. His old medical books and journals filled the tall bookcases on the inner wall. There was a worn couch and two comfy, faded easy chairs.

"Have a seat." Joleen closed the door.

The Atwoods did not sit.

They stood in the center of the room, between the couch and her father's desk. Robert looked more severe than ever. And Antonia, hovering in his shadow as always, looked nothing short of bleak—too pale, her thin brows drawn together. She had clasped her hands in front of her. The knuckles were dead white.

Joleen said, "Antonia? Are you all right?"

"Oh, yes. Fine. Just fine…"

"But you don't look "

Robert interrupted, "My wife says she is fine."

"Well, I know, but—"

"Please. I have something of real importance to propose to you now. I'll need your undivided attention."

Joleen did not get it. Antonia looked positively stricken, and all her husband could think about was what he wanted to say? A sarcastic remark rose to her lips. She bit it back. "All right. What is it, Mr. Atwood?"

Robert cleared his throat. "Joleen, after the spectacle I have witnessed today, I find I cannot keep quiet any longer. I have come to a difficult but important decision. It is painfully obvious to me that my grandson cannot get the kind of upbringing he deserves while he is in your care. Antonia and I are prepared to take him off your hands. I'm willing to offer you five hundred thousand dollars to sign over custody of young Samuel to me."

Chapter Three

Joleen forgot all about Antonia's distress. She could feel her blood pressure rising. So much for trying to make it work with the Atwoods.

She spoke through gritted teeth. "I'm sorry. I'm sure I could not have heard you right. You did not just offer to *buy* my baby from me—did you?"

Antonia squeaked. There was no other word for it, for that small, desperate, anguished sound. She squeaked and then she just stood there, wringing her hands.

Robert, however, had no trouble forming words. "Buy your baby? What an absurd suggestion. Of course, I'm not offering to *buy* Samuel. What I *am* offering you is a chance. A chance to do the right thing. For your child. And for yourself, as well."

"The right thing?" Joleen echoed in sheer disbelief. "To sell you my baby is the *right thing?*"

Robert waved a hand, a gesture clearly intended to erase her question as if it had never been. "I know that you have never attended college—except for a year, wasn't it, at some local trade school?"

"Who told you that?"

"I have my sources. Now you will be able to finish your education. You'll be able to do more with your life than run a beauty shop."

"I happen to like running a beauty shop."

He looked vaguely outraged, as if she had just told an insulting and rude lie. "Please."

"It's true. I love the work that I do."

He refused to believe such a thing. "I am offering you a *future,* Joleen. You are a young, healthy woman. You will have other children. My son only had one. Antonia and I want a chance to bring that one child up properly."

"Meaning *I* won't bring Sam up properly."

"My dear Joleen, you are twisting what I've said."

"I am not twisting anything. I am laying it right on the line. You don't think I will bring my son up right, so you want to *buy* him from me."

"You are overdramatizing."

Joleen, who, since the loss of her kind and steady father a decade before, had always been the calmest person in her family, found it took all of her will not to start shrieking—not to grab the brass paperweight on her father's desk and toss it right in Robert Atwood's smug face.

"My offer is a good one," Robert Atwood said.

Joleen gaped at him. "I beg your pardon. It is never a good offer when you try to buy someone's child."

"Joleen—"

"And what is the matter with you, anyway? Your 'offer' is bad enough all by itself. But couldn't you have waited a day or two? Did you have to come at me on my sister's wedding day?"

"Please…" croaked Antonia. She looked as if she might cry.

Robert put his arm around her—to steady her or to silence her, Joleen wasn't sure which. He held his proud white head high. "Once we'd made the decision, the sooner the better was the way it seemed to me. Might as well make our position clear. Might as well get you thinking along the right track."

A number of furious epithets rose to Joleen's lips. She did not utter a one of them—but she would, if this man went on saying these awful things much longer.

This conversation can only go downhill, she thought. Better to end it now.

"Mr. Atwood, I'm afraid if you stay very much longer, I will say some things that I'll be sorry for. I would like you to leave now."

Antonia made another of those squeaky little noises. Robert squeezed her shoulder and said to Joleen, "I want you to think about what I've said."

I am not going to start yelling at this man, she told herself silently. She said, "I do not have to think about it. The answer is no. You cannot have my child. Not at any price."

Robert Atwood stood even taller, if that was possible. "My dear, I would advise you not to speak without thinking."

"Stop calling me that. I am not your dear."

"Joleen, I am trying to make certain that you understand your position here."

Joleen blinked. This had to be a nightmare, didn't it? It could not be real. "My position?"

"Yes. You are an unwed mother."

Unwed mother. The old-fashioned phrase hurt. It made her sound cheap—and irresponsible, too. Not to mention a little bit stupid. Someone who hadn't had sense enough to get a ring on her finger before she let a man into her bed.

Maybe, she admitted to herself, it hurt because it was all too true. She had not been smart when it came to Bobby Atwood. Which seemed funny, at that moment. Funny in a sharp and painful way. A tight laugh escaped her.

"Don't try to make light of this, Joleen."

The urge to laugh vanished as quickly as it had come. "I promise you, Mr. Atwood, I am not makin' light. Not in the least."

"Good. For child care, you rely on your family members, and they are not the kind of people who should be caring for my grandson."

Joleen thought of that paperweight again—of how good it would feel to grab it and let it fly. "You better watch yourself, insultin' my family."

Robert Atwood shrugged. "I am merely stating facts. Your mother, from what I understand, and from what I witnessed today, is sexually promiscuous. Your younger sister has been in serious trouble at school and was arrested last year in a shoplifting incident. Your other sister has had some problems with the law, as well. None of those three—your mother or those sisters of yours, are the kind I would trust around my grandson. If it comes down to it, I will have little trouble convincing a judge that females like that aren't fit caregivers for Samuel, that he would be much better off with Antonia and me.''

Joleen couldn't help it. She raised her voice. '' 'Females like that'?'' she cried. ''Just who do you think you are, to call my family *females like that?*''

''You are shouting,'' said Robert Atwood.

''You're darn right I am. I was warned about you and I should have listened. But I didn't, and look what has happened.''

''Joleen—''

''That is all. That is it. You won't get my baby, don't think that you will. And I want you out of my mother's house.''

Right then the door to the front hall swung inward. It was Dekker, all six foot three and 220, or so, very muscular pounds of him. ''Joleen. Everything okay?''

The sight of her dear friend calmed her—at least a little. She said quietly, ''Everything's fine. The Atwoods were just leaving.''

''You'll be hearing from my attorney,'' Robert Atwood said.

''Fine. Just go. Now.''

Apparently, he'd said all he came to say. At last. With great dignity he guided his wife toward the door.

Which Dekker was blocking. ''What's this about a lawyer?'' he demanded.

Robert Atwood spoke to Joleen. ''Tell this thug to step out of my way.''

Joleen longed to tell Dekker just the opposite—to ask him if he would please break both of the Atwoods in two. But, no. It wouldn't be right to kill the At-woods. Not on DeDe's wedding day, anyway.

"It's okay, Dekker. Let them go."

Dekker, who had a fair idea of what had been going on in Samuel's study, stepped aside reluctantly. The Atwoods left the room. He followed them, just to make certain they got the hell out.

Once they went through the front door, he shut it firmly behind them. Then he returned to Joleen.

She was standing by her father's desk, a pretty woman in a long dress that was not quite pink and not quite red. Her heart-shaped face was flushed, her full mouth tight. A frown had etched itself between those big brown DuFrayne eyes.

Dekker quietly closed the door.

Her mouth loosened enough to quiver a little. "Please don't say 'I told you so.'"

Just to make sure he had it figured out, he said, "They want to take Sam away from you."

He hoped that maybe she would tell him it wasn't so. But she didn't. She picked up a brass paperweight of a Yankee soldier on a rearing horse from the edge of Samuel's desk. "I thought about smashing Robert Atwood in the face with this."

Dekker shook his head. "Bad idea. And, anyway, violence is not your style."

"Right now I feel like it could be. I feel like I could do murder and never think twice."

"You couldn't."

She clutched the brass figure against her body and looked at him with fury in her eyes. "He called my mother *promiscuous,* Dekker. He said Mama and DeDe and Niki weren't fit to take care of Sam. He

raised a shallow, sweet-talkin' lowlife like Bobby—
God forgive me for speakin' ill of the dead—and he
has the nerve to come in my mother's house and say
that my people are not good enough to do right by my
child, that *I* am not good enough, that—''

In two long strides, he was at her side.

She looked at him with a kind of bewildered surprise—that he had moved so fast, or maybe that, in
moving, he had distracted her from her rage. ''What?''

''Better give me that.''

She only gripped the paperweight tighter. ''He offered me *money*, Dekker. Money for my baby. Five
hundred thousand dollars to let them have Sam.''

Dekker swore. ''I'm sorry, Jo. You shouldn't have
had to listen to garbage like that.'' He put his hand
over hers. ''Come on. Put this thing down....''

She allowed him to pry her fingers open. He set the
paperweight back in its place on the desk. Then he
took her by the shoulders.

''What else?'' he asked, when she finally met his
eyes.

She swallowed, shook her head as if to clear it of
so much hot, hurtful rage. ''When I...when I told him
no, that I wouldn't take his money and he could not
have my child, he started talkin' lawsuits, how he
would not have any trouble convincing a judge that
Sam would be better off living with him and Antonia.''

Predictable, thought Dekker. He said, ''Anything
more?''

Those big eyes narrowed. ''He knew. About how
Niki got picked up for shoplifting last year. And he

seemed to know about DeDe, about her little joyride in that stolen car.''

In fact, it was one of Niki's friends from the bad-news crowd she'd been hanging around who'd actually tried to walk out of the department store with a cashmere sweater under her coat. But Niki *had* been there. She had known of the attempted theft and done nothing to stop it. And before that, there had been a series of incidents at school, bad grades and detentions, minor vandalism of school property and truancies, too.

As for DeDe, between the ages of fifteen and eighteen, she had been a true wild child. She went out with bad boys, she drank, she experimented with drugs. She'd ended up before a judge after the incident with the car, when she'd hitched a ride with a boy she hardly knew. The boy had shared his bottle of tequila with her and taken her down I-35 at a hundred miles an hour.

She'd gotten off easy, because it was her first arrest and because she hadn't known that the car was stolen and because, by some miracle, the judge had believed her when she swore she hadn't known. But she'd come very close to doing some time. After that, she'd cleaned up her act.

The problem with Niki and DeDe, the way Dekker saw it, was losing their father—and not getting enough attention and supervision from their mother. Camilla loved her girls with all her heart, but she'd been sunk in desperate grief for the first year or two after Samuel's death. And since then she was often distracted by all the boyfriends. She also worked long hours at the salon that she and Joleen now operated together.

Joleen had done her best to pick up the slack, to be there for her sisters, to offer attention and to provide discipline. She'd taken a lot of flack from both DeDe and Niki for her pains. They'd acted out their resentments on her; they'd fought her every time she tried to rein them in.

But recently things had started looking up. Niki had left the bad crowd behind. She took school seriously, was getting As and Bs rather than Ds and Fs. And DeDe had really settled down, as well. Joleen had dared to let herself think that the worst part of raising her own sisters was behind her.

Not that the reform of the Tilly girls would matter one damn bit to a self-righteous bastard like Robert Atwood.

"Oh, I cannot believe this is happening." Joleen pulled away from Dekker's grip and sank to one of the faded easy chairs. For a moment, she stared down at her lap, slim shoulders drooping. Then she pulled herself up straight again. "When I asked him *how* he knew those things about my sisters and my mother, he said he had his *sources.* Dekker, that man has had someone snooping around in our lives." She said it as if it were some sort of surprise. "Why, I would not put it past him to have hired someone, some private detective..."

"You mean someone like me?"

She let out a small, guilty-sounding groan. "Oh, Dekker, no. I didn't mean it that way...."

"It's okay. *I* did. I'm damn good at what I do. When I dig up the dirt on someone for a client, I get it all. I'm sure whoever Robert Atwood hired has done the same."

She put up a hand to swipe a shiny golden-brown curl back from her forehead. "Dekker, it won't work, will it? He couldn't get Sam by claiming that my mother and sisters are unfit. Could he?"

Dekker wished he didn't have to answer that one.

Joleen picked up his reluctance. "You think it *could* work, don't you?" Her shoulders drooped again. "Oh, God…"

He dropped to a crouch at her feet. "Look. I'm only saying it *might* work. Your sisters and your mother all pitch in, to take care of Sam when you can't."

"So? Good child care costs plenty. If I had to hire someone, I couldn't come close to affording the kind of care I can get from my family for free." She leaned toward him in the chair, intent on convincing him of how right she was—though somewhere in the back of her mind, she had to realize she was preaching to the choir. "They are good with him, Dekker, you know that they are. And as for Niki and DeDe, it's been a long time since there's been any trouble from either of them. And Mama—well, all right. She likes men and she loves to go out. Is that a crime? I don't know all her secrets, but I know she is not having *affairs* with all of them. She is no bed hopper. She loves the romance of it, that's all. She loves getting flowers and going dancing. But then, after way too little time with each guy, she can't pretend anymore. She admits to herself that the latest man is not my father. So she moves on to the next one—and what in the world does that have to do with how she is with Sam?"

"It's got nothing to do with how she is with Sam. The truth is, Camilla is a fine grandma. You know it and I know it. But I'm trying to get you to see that it's not the truth that matters here.''

She blinked. ''Not the truth?''

''No, Jo,'' he said patiently. ''It's the way things look. The way Robert Atwood and the lawyers he gets will *make* things look. It's appearances. A war of words and insinuations. Atwood's lawyers will take what your sisters have actually done and make it look a hundred times worse. They'll leave out any extenuating circumstances, minimize things like recent good behavior. It will be their job to make it appear that DeDe and Nicole are a pair of hardened criminals. And they'll make your mama look like some kind of—''

Joleen put up a hand. ''Don't say it, okay? She's not. You know she's not.''

''That's right. I know. But my opinion doesn't count for squat here. You have to come to grips with that.''

She just didn't want to get it. So she launched into a renewed defense of Camilla and the girls. ''They're great with Sam, Dekker. All three of them. He is nuts about them, and they take wonderful care of him. They—''

''Joleen. Listen. The point is not what good care they take of Sam. The point is, what is a judge going to think?'' He caught her hands, chafed them between his own. ''If the Atwoods hired me to work up a negative report on Camilla and your sisters, I could get enough together to make them look pretty bad.''

She swallowed again and tugged her hands free of his. ''Oh, I hate this.''

Should he have left it at that? Maybe. But he had

to be sure she understood the true dimensions of the problem.

"Jo."

She made a small, unwilling noise in her throat.

He laid it on her. "There's also the little problem of Robert Atwood's influence in this town. He has power, Joleen. Lots of it. You have to face that. He's contributed to a hell of a lot of big-time political causes and campaigns, and he has supported the careers of a number of local judges."

"What are you tellin' me? That some judge is going to give my little boy to the Atwoods as payback on some political favor?"

"It could be a factor."

"Well, that's just plain wrong."

"It doesn't *matter* that it's wrong."

"But—"

"I keep trying to make you see. Right and wrong are not the issues here. It's money, Joleen. Money and power. You can't underestimate what big bucks and heavy-duty influence can do."

She swiped that cute brown curl off her forehead again. "Oh, why didn't I listen to you? I never should have called him. I never should have—"

"But you did. And even though I thought it was a bad idea, I do know that you did it for the right reasons. For Sam's sake. And to give the Atwoods a chance to know their grandson."

"It was also pride, Dekker," she said in a small voice. "I've got...a problem with pride. I want to do right. I want to do right so bad, I get pigheaded about it. And I, well, it's exactly what you said earlier. I'm ashamed. I was supposed to be the one with both of my feet on the ground in this family. But look at me…''

He couldn't help reaching out and running a finger along her soft cheek. ''You look just fine.''

She caught his hand, squeezed it, let it go. ''You know what I mean. I ended up with a baby and no husband, got myself 'in trouble,' made the oldest mistake in the book. So when I called Robert Atwood, I was hopin'…to make up for that, somehow. To be bigger than the mess I got myself into. To get past my own bad judgment in falling for Bobby by reachin' out to his folks in their hour of need. It was pride, Dekker. You were right. Just plain old pigheaded pride.''

''And now it's over and done with. You need to let it go and move on.''

''How can I let it go when I am so *furious* at myself?''

''Look at it this way. It's very likely, even if you hadn't told them they had a grandson, that the Atwoods would have found out about Sam eventually. We may not travel in their circles. But word does get around.''

''You really think so?''

''Yeah.'' He rose to stand above her. ''Now. Are you finished giving yourself hell?''

She blew out a long breath. ''Oh, I guess.''

''Then we can start thinking about what to *do,* about how to fight what they're going to be throwing at you. The main attack is going to be on the fitness of your child care, the way it looks now.''

She stared up at him. ''What are you telling me?''

''I think you know.''

For an endless few moments, neither of them spoke. Noises from outside the study rose up to fill the quiet—a woman's laughter beyond the high leaded-glass window that looked out on the side of the house, the music on Camilla's stereo, something slow and bluesy and sweet.

"All right," Joleen said at last. "I'll find someone else to watch Sam when I'm working. It will be tight, but I'll manage it."

"Good."

"And then somehow I will have to tell my mama and my sisters why they are suddenly not to be trusted with the little boy they all adore."

"You don't have to tell them anything tonight. You've got a little time to think it over. You'll come up with a good approach."

"It doesn't matter what approach I take, there will be hurt feelings. There will be cryin' and carryin' on— and then I've got to get a good lawyer, right?"

"Yes. But don't worry there. I'll find you the right man."

"And then I have to *pay* the lawyer. Oh, what a mess. There is no way around it. This is going to cost a bundle."

Dekker knew that Joleen made an okay living, working with her mother. She supported herself and Sam and she did a decent job of it. He also knew that there wasn't much left over once all the bills were paid. Quality child care and a good lawyer would stretch her budget way past the breaking point.

But it was okay. Money, after what had happened in Los Angeles, would be the least of their problems.

Dekker wanted to tell her as much. However, that would only get her started asking questions about L.A.

Right now, they had a limited amount of time before someone would be knocking on the study door, demanding that Joleen get out there and deal with some other minor crisis. When he told her about L.A., he didn't want to be interrupted.

"Don't look so miserable," he said. "We're just getting it all out there, so we can see what we have to deal with."

"I know." But she didn't know. He could see by her worried frown that the money problem was really bothering her.

He strove to ease her fears without saying too much. "The money issue can be handled."

"I don't see how." She looked down at her lap and shook her head.

"Jo, I'll help out. The bills will get paid."

"Oh, no." She glanced up then, her frown deeper than before. "You work hard for your money. And we both know you don't have much more of it than I do."

Joleen was right—or she would have been right, as of a few days ago. Before the trip to Southern California, Dekker would have had to rob a bank to be of much use to her financially. He'd gone into something of a downward spiral, right after his wife, Stacey, died. He'd quit his job and sold his house. He had not worked for several months while grief and guilt did their best to eat him alive. With Joleen's help, he'd pulled himself out of it. But by that time he didn't have a whole hell of a lot left.

For almost two years now he had operated a one-man detective agency in a one-room office over a coin laundry downtown. It paid the rent and put food on the table, but that was about it.

Or it had been. Until he'd flown to L.A. and learned that he had money to burn. He was a rich man now, and he had every intention of spending whatever it took to help Joleen fight the SOB who thought he could take her child away.

"I have a few extra resources," he said. "I mean it. Don't worry about money."

"Dekker. You are not listening."

"No. *You're* the one who's not listening."

"I couldn't take money from you."

"Sure you could—for Sam's sake."

"No. It wouldn't be right. I couldn't live with myself if I—"

Someone knocked on the door. "Joly?" It was DeDe's voice. "Joly, are you in there?"

Joleen glanced toward the sound and sighed.

Dekker said softly, "It's all right. We'll talk more. Later. After the party's over and everyone's gone home."

"You know that's going to be good and late."

"It's okay. I'll be available."

"Thank you," she said. Even if he hadn't been a brand-new multimillionaire, the look she gave him then would have made him feel like one.

"Joly?" DeDe knocked again.

Joleen pushed herself from the chair and smoothed out her skirt. "Come on in."

The door swung inward and DeDe demanded, "What are you doing in here? I have been looking all over for you."

"Well, you have found me."

DeDe glanced from her sister to Dekker, then back to Joleen again. "What's going on?"

Dekker laughed. "None of your business. What do you need?"

DeDe wrinkled her nose. "Oh, it's Uncle Stan. He wants some *special* coffee." In the Tilly and Du-Frayne families, *special* coffee was coffee dosed with Irish Cream and Grand Marnier.

"And?" Joleen prompted.

"I can't find the Bailey's."

"Did you look in the—"

DeDe groaned. "I looked *everywhere*. Would you just come and find it?"

"Sure."

"And it's almost eight. I think I should throw the bouquet pretty soon."

"Good idea."

"I want you to stand about ten feet, in a direct line, behind me when I do it. Understand?"

"DeDe." Joleen looked weary. "The whole idea with the bouquet is that everyone is supposed to get a fair chance at it."

"Too bad. It's my wedding. And my big sister is catchin' my bouquet."

Chapter Four

Joleen did catch the bouquet.

It wasn't as if she had a choice in the matter. DeDe, after all, had made up her mind that Joleen would be getting it. And there was just no sense fighting DeDe once she'd made up her mind.

Cousin Callie Tilly, one of Uncle Stan's daughters, who worked at Local Oklahoma Bank and had just hit the big three-oh with no prospective husband in sight, was a little put out at the way DeDe went and tossed those flowers at the exact spot where Joleen stood. Callie grumbled that she was older than Joleen and she needed that bouquet more.

But her own father told her to quit whining and have herself a little *special* coffee. Which cousin Callie did. And then one of Wayne's friends, a handsome cowboy in dress jeans and fancy tooled boots, asked Callie if she would care to dance. Her attitude improved considerably after that.

Joleen put Sam to bed upstairs in her old room at a little after nine o'clock. When she went back outside, she did some dancing herself. She danced with Uncle Stan and Bud and Burly. And with another friend of Wayne's, a tall, broad-shouldered fellow who ran an oyster bar in Tulsa. He told her she had beautiful eyes and that she knew how to follow. He claimed there were way too many women who tried to lead when they danced. Joleen smiled sweetly up at him and wondered if he was casting some kind of aspersion on modern women as a whole.

Then she decided she was just too suspicious. A guy called her a good dancer and she started thinking of ways to take it as an offense.

But then again, after what had happened with Bobby Atwood two years ago and with Bobby's father just this evening, well, was it any wonder she had trouble trusting men?

After the oyster bar owner from Tulsa, she danced with Dekker. Thank God for Dekker. Now there was a man that a woman could trust. She was so very fortunate to have a friend like him, who came straight to her aid anytime things got tough.

Of course, she would never take the money he insisted he would give her. But it meant the world, that he would offer—and that he always came through for her and her mama and her sisters, too.

Anytime any one of them needed him, he was there.

And did she ever need him now. She needed his clear mind and his steely nerves—not to mention all he knew from being first a cop and now a private investigator. Dekker saw all the angles. Yes, he was way too cynical—but right now she needed someone who looked at the world through wide-open eyes. Someone to show her how to fight Bobby's father at his own game.

Joleen closed her eyes and laid her head on Dekker's broad shoulder.

"It's going to be all right, Jo," he whispered against her hair.

Something in his tone alerted her. She lifted her head and looked up at him. "You've thought of what to do. I can hear it in your voice."

"Could be."

She couldn't read his expression. "What *are* you thinking?"

"Later." He guided her head back to rest on his shoulder. "After everyone's gone home. We'll talk about it then. About *all* of it...."

At eleven DeDe and Wayne took off for Wayne's house. They'd spend their wedding night there and then leave in the morning for a twelve-day honeymoon at a two-hundred-year-old inn on the Mississippi shore.

Wayne's new peacock-green SUV had been properly adorned for the occasion, with Just Married scrawled in shaving cream across the rear window, Here Comes the Bride on the windshield and tin cans hooked to the rear bumper by lengths of thick string.

Joleen had the bird seed ready, wrapped in little rose-colored satin squares and tied with white bows. She passed it around and DeDe and Wayne ducked through a rain of it as they raced for the car. Then everyone stood on the sidewalk beneath the Victorian-style lamps that lined all the streets of Mesta Park, waving and calling out last-minute advice.

''Good luck!''

''Don't do anything we wouldn't do!''

''But if you do, take pictures!''

Wayne revved the engine and pulled away from the curb. The handsome SUV rolled off into the night, tin cans rattling behind.

Most of the guests took their leave then, turning for their own cars, waving goodbye and making happy noises about what a great time they'd had. A few stayed on—Callie and her cowboy, one of Camilla's admirers, Aunt LeeAnne and Uncle Foley—to enjoy another dance or two out in the lantern-lit backyard. It was after one when Camilla, Joleen and Dekker showed the last of them to the door.

'''Bye, now. Drive with care....'' Camilla shut the door, turned off the porch light and then stretched like a sleek and very contented cat. ''Oh, it has been a long and lovely day.'' Her smooth brows drew together. ''Now, where did Niki get off to?''

Joleen said, ''She went up to bed about half an hour ago.''

''Our little Sammy all snuggled in?''

''I put him down in my room.''

''Well.'' Camilla gave her oldest daughter a lazy smile. ''I believe I am ready for bed myself. You and Sammy stayin'?''

''I think so. I'd just as soon not wake him. And tomorrow I'd only be headin' back over here to start cleaning up.''

"Good. You'll lock the doors when you're through down here, then?"

"I will. Right now, though, Dekker and I are goin' out in back for a while, to enjoy the peace and quiet."

"Don't you start in cleaning up tonight," Camilla warned. "I mean it. It's late. You've worked hard enough. We'll take care of everything tomorrow."

"I won't lift a finger, I promise."

Camilla was not convinced. She shook her head and clucked her tongue. "I know how you are. The only child of mine who will work instead of playin' if given the choice. You have to learn to slow down a little, baby. Smell the flowers now and then."

"Mama, I'm not cleaning up a thing tonight. We're just going to sit outside and talk some, that's all."

"What do you two talk about? Always with your heads together. Thick as thieves, I swear."

"Nothing important, Mama." Well, all right. That was a flat-out lie. But the truth, right then, would not have served. When the time came, Joleen would tell her mother whatever she thought her mother had to know.

Camilla was already on her way up the stairs. She paused on the third step and cast a glance toward the door to the living room. Uncle Hubert was still in there, snoring away. They could hear the low rumblings even through the closed door. "Put a blanket over Hubert?"

"I will. Right away. 'Night, Mama."

"'Night..." Camilla went on up.

Joleen got a chenille throw from the closet under the stairs. She and Dekker spread it over Uncle Hubert, who just went on snoring, gone to the world.

"You want a beer or something?" she asked Dekker before they went outside.

"I wouldn't mind some ice water."

That sounded good to her, too, so she fixed them two tall glasses and led him out into the night.

Camilla had a matching pair of chaise lounges with nice, thick, floral-patterned cushions. For the wedding party, Joleen had put them near the fence, under the sweet gum in the corner of the yard. A low patio table sat between the lounges, just perfect for setting their glasses on.

"You think it's too dark out here?" Joleen asked. They'd unplugged the lanterns a little while before.

"I like the dark."

So they went over and stretched out on the lounges and stared up through the leaves of the sweet gum at the stars. They hadn't had a single frost yet, so cicadas serenaded them from the trees, making it seem as though it was still summer. Now and then, from the wires overhead, night birds trilled out their high, lonesome songs. The moon had gone down some time before, but as her eyes adjusted, Joleen found she could see well enough, after all. There were no clouds, and the stars were like diamonds sewn into the midnight fabric of the sky.

Joleen set her glass down and leaned back, aware of a jittery feeling in her stomach. Anticipation. She just knew that her friend had come up with a way out of this tight spot she had got herself into.

He had said as much, hadn't he?

Everything will be all right, Jo. Dekker was not the kind to give her empty words. If he said things would be all right, it was because he honestly thought they would be.

She waited, her jitters increasing, wishing she could see inside his mind, that she could know what he was thinking, what kind of plan he had thought up—and at the same time reticent, not wanting to push him, feeling it was only right he should say what he had to say in his own time. And in his own way.

He sipped his ice water, set it down next to hers. And then, finally, he spoke. "I want to tell you about Los Angeles first."

Oh, not now, she thought. She did want to hear about whatever had gone on out there, but right now, as far as she was concerned, everything took a back seat to the problem of Robert Atwood and the threat he posed to Sam.

Be patient, she silently reminded herself as she sucked in a slow breath and let it out with care. "All right. Tell me about Los Angeles."

It was a moment before he said anything. Cicada songs swelled, then faded off when he spoke.

"Do you remember, about a week and a half ago, that couple who showed up at your mama's front door—Jonas Bravo and his wife, Emma?"

Joleen remembered. Jonas Bravo and his wife had told a strange story about a baby, a baby that had been Jonas Bravo's younger brother. They'd claimed that the baby had been kidnapped thirty years ago. And that they were looking for a Lorraine Smith, who was supposed to know something about the kidnapping. Joleen had told them that the Lorraine Smith who used to live next door wasn't going to be able to help them, since she was no longer alive. Then Camilla had mentioned that Lorraine had a son. As soon as they heard that, they'd asked to speak with Dekker. Camilla had suggested they try him at work.

Joleen sought her friend's eyes through the darkness. "I thought you said it was nothing. That they were mistaken—that it must have been some other Lorraine Smith they were looking for."

"I lied."

She considered that admission for a moment, then asked, "Well, and why did you go and do that?"

"Because I didn't want to deal with what they'd told me. I didn't want to think about it and I didn't want to talk about it, either."

"You mean you were lyin' to *yourself?*"

"That's right."

The little hairs on the back of Joleen's neck were standing at attention. "You're saying that your mama did know something about a kidnapped baby?"

He made a low noise, a noise that meant yes.

"So when Jonas Bravo and his wife showed up at your office…"

"They told me about the baby, Jonas's younger brother. And I told them I didn't know anything about any baby, and neither had my mother. I asked them to leave. And they did."

"Okay. But I don't see what—"

"I left out a few details, when I told you about it—like the fact that Jonas said he believed *I* was the baby."

Joleen's mouth felt dry. She picked up her ice water and knocked back a big gulp. "Wait a minute. Jonas Bravo said that *you* were the kidnapped baby?"

"Right."

"The kidnapped baby who was Jonas's brother?"

Dekker was nodding at her. "Jonas said he believed that I had been kidnapped by 'our' uncle, Blake Bravo, for revenge against his own brother, Jonas's father."

"Revenge? Why?"

"That's a whole other story. Evidently, Blake was a real shady character, had been disinherited. He blamed his brother for it. So he came up with this scheme to kidnap his younger nephew and hold the baby for ransom. He had an accomplice, according to Jonas."

"Not…Lorraine?"

"Yes, Lorraine."

Joleen had that feeling again, the one she'd had in her father's study when Robert Atwood had told her he would take her child from her: that feeling of stark unreality—the absolute certainty this couldn't be real. "This is crazy. Lorraine was your *mother*. We all know that."

"Not according to Jonas Bravo. He told me that the woman I'd always believed to be my mother had helped Blake Bravo kidnap me. That Blake had demanded—and got—two million dollars worth of diamonds as a ransom."

"Two *million?* Whoa. The Bravos must have had plenty of money."

"They did. And they *still* do. Jonas manages the Bravo holdings. He's an excellent businessman. They call him the Bravo Billionaire."

Joleen took another swallow of ice water. "They?"

"The newspapers, the scandal sheets. Bravo is an important name in Los Angeles." Dekker was watching her. He waited till she set her glass down again before he said, "So Blake got the diamonds—but he never returned the baby he had kidnapped. He and Lorraine disappeared, along with that baby, never to be seen or heard from again."

"The baby that was…you?" It all seemed so incredible.

"Right. That's what Jonas claimed."

"And you denied it."

"Yes. I said it wasn't true and I asked him and Emma to leave. But I couldn't stop thinking about the things that he'd said. I remembered my mother's diary."

This was more news to Joleen. "Lorraine left a diary?"

"Yes. She asked me not to read it until she was gone. I put it away. And I *never* read it. I guess I just didn't want to deal with what I would find in there. But after Jonas and his wife paid me that visit, I couldn't stop thinking about it. I dug it out of her things."

"And?"

"It contained her confession. She verified everything Jonas had told me. That she helped kidnap me as a baby and that she—well, she decided she wanted to keep me. She couldn't have kids of her own. She wrote that, from the moment she lifted me out of my crib, the night that they took me from the Bravo mansion, she knew she would never give me up. In the end, after several months of moving around, living under various aliases, Blake set her up with a new identity. And a house."

"The house…next door?"

"You got it."

"So that means Jonas Bravo..."

"*Is* my brother."

"And you took off for L.A. on Wednesday because—"

"As soon as I read what Lorraine wrote, I felt I had to go looking for him, to tell him what I'd found."

"Oh, Dekker." She reached across the distance between them and brushed his arm with her fingertips. "I'll bet you couldn't get there fast enough."

His white teeth flashed in the darkness as he gave her a smile. "I knew you'd understand."

"I do. I just...well, I can hardly believe it. You have a *brother*...." Which was wonderful, really. Finding out he had more family, to Joleen's mind, would be nothing but good for Dekker.

The part about Lorraine, though. That was just terrible. And so hard to accept.

Lorraine Smith had been a quiet woman, and a little bit shy, a person who tended to fade into the background in a crowd. Joleen had always thought of her as gentle. And good at heart.

Incredible, Joleen thought. Impossible.

Lorraine was not Dekker's mama, after all. Lorraine was a kidnapper, and Dekker was the baby that she stole.

She said, "I do wish you'd explained all this earlier. I got pretty worried. I thought all kinds of things, that you might be in danger..."

"I wasn't in danger. I just couldn't talk about it. Not then, when I first found out."

"I am not blaming you, Dekker. You did what you had to do. And that was to contact your brother and to share with him what you found."

"Which brings us around to the situation with Robert Atwood."

The quick shift in subject surprised her. For a few minutes there, with all this shocking news Dekker was laying on her, she'd actually forgotten Bobby's father and the threat he presented to Sam. "Wait a minute. What does your being Jonas Bravo's brother have to do with Robert Atwood?"

"Remember earlier I told you that money would be no problem?"

"Oh, Dekker, don't start with that again. I appreciate your offerin' to help out that way. It means so much that you would, but I told you, I cannot allow you to—"

"Jo, I'm a rich man now."

Her mouth was open, since he'd cut her off in the middle of a sentence. She shut it, then opened it again to say, "Huh?"

"The Bravos never gave up on the idea that I might be alive somewhere. Arrangements were made for me, a huge trust set aside, just in case I might someday show up again."

His words made her head spin. "Arrangements...a huge trust?"

"Right. What I'm trying to say is, I have millions, Joleen."

There was that word again. Millions. Millions in diamonds. And also... "Millions of *dollars?*"

"What else?"

"Well, I don't know. I can't...Dekker, are you serious? You are a *millionaire?*"

"I am serious, Jo. I am a millionaire." He was grinning again.

"Well. I can't...I don't..."

He chuckled. "You are sputtering."

"It's just...so much to take in all at once. Oh, what a crazy day it has been."

"It's not over yet."

She peered at him suspiciously. "There's more?"

"You bet. There's my solution to your problem."

That made her smile. "I knew it."

"Knew what?"

"That you had come up with a way to get me out of this mess."

"And I have. It came to me a few hours ago, while we were dancing. Like a bolt right out of the blue. You're going to think it's insane at first. But give me a chance, let me convince you."

"Dekker. What? Convince me of what?"

"I want you to marry me, Jo."

Chapter Five

Joleen discovered that she understood the true meaning of the words, *struck speechless*.

Dekker chuckled again.

And Joleen found she could talk, after all. "It's a joke, right? You are makin' a joke."

"It's no joke, Jo."

"Well, but you are grinnin'. And what was that sound I just heard coming out of your mouth? If that wasn't a laugh, I will eat that bouquet my sister made me catch tonight."

"Sorry." He took pains to arrange his expression into more serious lines. "I couldn't help it. You should have seen the look on your face. Like that time when you were…oh, about eight, I think. And that kid from up the block poured crushed ice down your pants."

Joleen was thinking that sometimes she wished she

hadn't known Dekker all her life. He remembered too many things she would just as soon forget.

He asked, "What was that kid's name?"

"Foster Stutterheim. I hated him."

"I think he had a thing for you."

"Well, and didn't he have a fine way of showing it?"

"He got your attention. You have to admit that."

"That's right, he did. I never spoke to him again."

"You were always way too hard on your admirers."

She thought of her one big mistake. "Not always."

Dekker's eyes gleamed at her. "Well, okay. There *was* Bobby Atwood."

"And I was *not* hard on him, and look where it got me."

He made a low noise in his throat. "Don't."

"What?"

"Don't start beating yourself up again."

"I won't."

"Good. We're dealing in solutions here."

"Right—and I still don't believe what you said a minute ago. Maybe you didn't say it. Maybe I just imagined it."

"I said it. And I want you to consider it."

"But Dekker, *why?* I mean, what good would our getting married do?"

"A lot. Remember, this is about appearances. About how things *look.* And it always looks better if a woman is not raising her child on her own. It looks better if she's married—and don't start making faces. I didn't say it was fair. I didn't say it was right. I didn't even say it was *true* that a married woman will necessarily be a better parent than an unmarried one. I'm just saying that people—and judges *are* people—tend to think of a two-parent home as the best thing for a kid.''

''Well, I understand that, but—''

''Wait. I said I wanted a chance to convince you, remember?''

She nodded.

''Then will you let me finish doing that?''

''Sorry.''

He continued, ''I'm a rich man now. And if we're married, you're not going to be giving me any of that 'I can't take your money' talk. My money will be your money. One of Robert Atwood's arguments will be that he can provide for his grandson better than you can. If you're married to me, that argument is shot down.''

''But, Dekker—''

He stopped her with a look. ''I also want you to consider what's been bothering you the most. Which is how you're going to afford both good child care *and* the legal battle that's coming up. If you marry me, the cost of all that will be no problem. You can hire the best damn lawyers, and you'll be able to pay for top quality child care. Hell, if you want to stop working altogether, be there full-time for Sam, you could do that, too.''

''Oh, I don't think so. You know me. I *like* to work.''

''Does that mean I've convinced you?''

She wasn't ready to admit *that* yet. ''I only said I like to work.''

''So fine. Work. And put Sam in the best day care center in the city.''

She had to admit that his arguments made sense.

But there were a few issues he hadn't covered—awkward, uncomfortable issues. Issues she felt a little bit embarrassed to bring up, even with her very best friend.

But still, they were issues that needed discussing before they did anything so wild and strange as to marry each other in order to keep Robert Atwood from taking her child.

"Say it," he said after a few very long minutes in which neither of them had made a sound. "Whatever it is, we can't deal with it if you won't get it out there."

She scrunched up her nose at him. "Well, I know that."

"Okay, then. Talk."

"It's just…"

"What?"

She stared at him, struck by the tone of his voice. He sounded…so excited about this. In the soft glow of starlight he looked eager and intent, his eyes focused hard on her, watching her so closely.

Such earnestness surprised her.

Most of the time it was hard to know what Dekker Smith was feeling. It wasn't that he *hid* his emotions, exactly. Just that he guarded them. He kept them in check. He could be warm and funny and gentle and kind. But most of the time he made it seem as though nothing was life-or-death to him. As if he could turn and walk away from anything, that there was nothing—and no one—he really *needed* to get by.

Of course, she had learned a few years ago how

deep his feelings actually went. It had almost killed him when Stacey died.

But still, he didn't make a habit of letting what was going on inside him show.

Not so right now.

Now he did seem eager. And earnest. And excited. Three words that, until that moment, she would never have used to describe Dekker Smith.

"Jo." His voice was gruff. "What *is* it? Damn it, talk to me."

She made herself say it. "It's just that, while I do love you and I know that you love me, it is not a man-and-woman kind of love. I guess I'm saying, what *about* love, Dekker? And, well, what about sex?"

He sent her a look of great patience. "Let's tackle one insurmountable obstacle at a time, all right?"

"Please don't make light. I think this is important."

"I didn't say it wasn't."

"But you—"

"I only meant that we'll work it out. Day by day, as we go along."

"Well, Dekker, I'm sorry. But I just can't."

"You can't take it day by day?"

"No, I mean I wouldn't feel right unless we came to some kind of understanding about what we're going to do when it comes to…the things that men and women do—and why are you looking at me like you find me *amusing?*"

"Because I do find you amusing—in a good way."

"Oh. In a good way, huh?"

"Yeah."

"That's supposed to make it all right that you are laughin' at me?"

"I am not laughing at you."

She made a humphing sound. "Well, I don't care. Whatever you're doing, it's not going to stop me from talkin' about this. Sex is a problem, and we have to face it."

"I disagree. Sex is *not* a problem. Not right now, anyway, not unless you insist on *making* it a problem."

"But…well, I mean, that's just not *us,* it's not what we are together. We are deep and true friends. But we are not lovers."

"Right. So?"

"Well, even if we didn't sleep together, if I was married to you, I would be *true* to you. And I would really hate it if you were not true to me. Marriage, even a marriage for practical reasons, is still a sacred trust, Dekker. A trust that should be respected and…" She could see that he was only waiting for his turn to talk. Fine. "What?" she demanded. "Say it. Go ahead."

"I would be true to you."

"You would?"

"Yes."

"But what if you—"

"Don't start in with the thousand and one possible reasons I might have for wanting to sleep around. I don't need to hear them. I said, I'll be true to you, even though we're not lovers."

"But what happens when—"

He cut her off, his voice low. "Fact is, it's just not that important to me."

She felt her cheeks warming. "It's not?"

"Right. It's not."

Maybe she had misunderstood him. "You mean, uh, you're telling me that *sex* is not that important to you?"

"Sex. Love—what you call man-and-woman love, anyway. When it comes to that, well, I'm pretty much dead meat."

Dead meat. How sad. Joleen had known that what had happened with Stacey had scarred her friend in a deep way. But she'd been telling herself he was slowly getting over the pain of that time.

Not so, evidently.

He went on. "I'd rather be with you than with a lover anyday. And I never planned to marry again— at least not until I thought of marrying you tonight. I've got to tell you, Jo. I like this idea. A marriage to you sounds damn good to me. Hell. To be legally a part of the family—of *your* family, and Sam's— sounds pretty terrific, as a matter of fact. Until you brought it up, I didn't even think of the sex issue. It didn't seem important. I guess I had some idea that, since Bobby Atwood did a number on you, you felt more or less the same way I do about love and romance and everything that goes with it."

Joleen found herself wondering, *did* she feel the same way—emotional dead meat when it came to man-woman love?

Well…

Not really.

"Oh, Dekker…"

He was sitting very still. "I'm listening."

She strove for just the right words. "I, well, I can see how you would think I don't want anything to do with love. The family drives me crazy, always after me to find someone, always telling me my turn for true love is comin' right up. Lately it seems like every wedding I go to, I'm the one who gets the bride's bouquet tossed in her face.''

"They do it because they want the best for you," he reminded her gently.

"I know they do. I know all their hearts are in the right places. But still, it aggravates me no end. It's like the old saying goes. Once burned, twice shy. Bobby did burn me. Bad. I just don't want a thing to do with it—with love and romance—not right now.''

"But?"

"Well, to you, Dekker, at this moment, because of the seriousness of what we are considering, I am willin' to admit something."

"Do it."

"Even on the day that Bobby turned his back on me, even then, when I had to face the fact that I'd made a worse mistake in judgment than my mama and my sisters ever made. Even then, I knew deep in my heart that someday—maybe not for years and years—but *someday* I would try again."

He looked at her levelly. "Years and years, Jo. Do you hear yourself? You are talking about a *long* time."

"Maybe so. But still. Someday, I can't help but hope, I will find love—and I mean the real and lastin' kind."

"Too bad you need a husband right now. A husband with a fat wallet, a husband you can count on."

"Well, okay. You may be right, but—"

"Let me put it this way." He leaned closer. They'd been talking quietly, but right then, he lowered his voice even more, as if they were a pair of conspirators, as if he were about to suggest the most dangerous conspiracy of all. "You could marry me now. We could deal with the Atwoods together, present a united front. And eventually, once the Atwoods are no longer a threat to you and Sam, if you feel you've got to have more than I can give you, well then, we'll end it."

She hated to say the ugly word, but it did require saying. "Divorce, you mean?"

He nodded.

She found herself leaning toward him as he leaned toward her. "So. We could marry..." She was whispering, too, keeping her voice way down low so that only he could hear, though it was nearing two in the morning and they were alone in her mother's dark backyard. "We could marry and live together and be just what we are—friends, and that's all. But we'd also stay true, to each other. Respect our vows. And then, if the time comes when one of us wants more than the other can give, we would get ourselves a divorce."

He nodded again. "That's exactly right."

She thought of the family. "What would we tell everyone? Would we try to make them think that all of a sudden the two of us discovered we were in love?"

"However you want to handle it. Maybe calling it love would be the best way to go. You've got some pretty big talkers in your family."

He had a point there. She said, "Aunt LeeAnne comes immediately to mind."

"That she does. And it's possible, if we let it be known that this marriage is really for Sam's sake, the Atwoods might get hold of that information. They could twist it to make it look as if there's no real commitment between us, as if it's only a marriage on paper, entered into so that you wouldn't lose Sam to them.''

"Well. And that would be the truth, more or less, wouldn't it?"

His gaze did not waver. "There is, always has been and always will be, commitment between us."

Oh, he was so right. They did share a very deep commitment. She swallowed, gave a nod.

He said, "Let me put it this way. If you think the Atwoods have a right to that particular truth, then we probably don't need to be having this conversation."

She took his meaning. "Because we might as well not be married at all, if Robert Atwood is going to be able to call our marriage a sham. That's what you're saying, right?"

He nodded.

"Okay." She flopped back against the cushion and stared up through the trees at the starry night sky. "So we'd need to make everyone think it's a real marriage, in every way. We'd need to—"

He chuckled again. "Jo. Settle down."

"Well, I want to get this all straight in my mind. I want to know exactly how we would manage everything."

"And I'm trying to tell you that we don't need to 'make' them think anything. We'll just say we love each other and we've decided to get married. I don't see why we have to go into any big explanations about what *kind* of love it is."

Easy for him to say. She sat up a little straighter. "Maybe *you* won't. You're the man. The women in my family will not be askin' you why, all of a sudden, you're getting hitched to your best friend.''

''You can handle them.''

''How?''

''Let them ask. Answer with care.''

She knew he had the right idea. But she did hate evading and telling lies. If she and Dekker did this, she would have to lie at least a little and evade a whole lot.

She told him, ''The family *will* have to know that the Atwoods are after Sam. Eventually, when we get to court, I don't see any way we could hide it. And then there's the baby-sitting issue. I'm going to have to tell my mama and my sisters why they suddenly can't watch my child.''

''Our getting married will make that easier.''

''How?''

''We'll tell them about the money I've got now, money that means you can start paying for day care, so you won't have to take advantage of them so much anymore.''

For the first time since they'd started this particular discussion, Joleen felt a smile curving her lips. ''Hey. When you say it that way, it doesn't sound bad at all.''

''And it's the truth, too.''

''Just not the *whole* truth.''

''Truth enough.''

Was it? Well, all right. Maybe it was.

He picked up his empty water glass. ''I think I wouldn't mind a beer, after all.''

''Help yourself.'' She gestured toward the coolers still lined up by the garden shed.

He rose from the chaise and went to get himself a

cold one. Joleen let her head drop back to the cushion again.

Strange. The more Dekker had talked, the more he had laid out all the reasons they ought to get married, the more his crazy idea seemed like the best way to handle her problem.

He was right about a lot of things.

Like when he said that neither of them was in the market for a grand passion right now—and that maybe neither of them would *ever* be. In that case the marriage could turn out to be just right for both of them, and in a forever way, too.

But however long it lasted, she felt certain they could make a go of it, make it work. Make a *good* marriage. Maybe there wouldn't be passion or even sex. But she had lived without sex and passion for a good part of her life. Going without those things hadn't killed her yet. And Dekker had just told her— and really seemed to mean it—that he could do without them, too.

Oh, and they did have so much that they shared. Yes, sometimes he was closemouthed, even with her. But she *never* kept secrets from him. She loved nothing so much as talking things over with him. And the thought of having him at her side, as her husband, when she faced the Atwoods, created the sweetest, most wonderful feeling of relief in her troubled heart.

He came back to her, stretched his big body out in the chaise next to hers again. She heard the popping sound as he opened his beer. She turned her head to him as he drank and watched him with fondness, waiting for him to look at her.

When he did meet her eyes, she spoke softly. "Thank you. For bein' my true friend."

He set the can on the low table between them. "Are you going to marry me?"

"Yes, Dekker. I am."

Chapter Six

They broke the news to the family the next day, at dinner. Uncle Stan and his wife, Aunt Catherine, were there. So were Bud and Burly. And Aunt LeeAnne and Uncle Foley. They'd all come by in the afternoon to help with the after-wedding cleanup.

Uncle Hubert was there, too. He had never left. He hadn't been much use as a worker, since he was nursing a sick hangover from his excesses the day before, but he came to the table when Camilla called him, so he heard the announcement right along with everyone else.

Niki cried. And so did Aunt LeeAnne.

"Oh, what did I tell you, hon?" Aunt LeeAnne sobbed. "I said you'd be next and wasn't I right?"

Joleen handed her aunt a tissue, gave her a hug, and agreed that yes, she had been right.

Uncle Hubert said, "This calls for a little drink, to celebrate."

Aunt LeeAnne sniffed. "The last thing anyone needs right now, Hubert, is a little drink."

Hubert, sober right then and at least somewhat abashed after his behavior at the wedding, had the grace not to argue with her. "Pass those little red pepper things," he mumbled.

They were having take-out. Camilla had ordered five giant-size deep-dish meat-lover's-style pizzas to feed the hungry cleanup crew.

Niki grabbed a tissue of her own and blew her nose. Then she reached for another big slice. "Oh, I can't believe it," she sniffled and swiped at her still-leaking eyes. "Dekker and Joly…married. Dekker will be like my brother for real…."

There were more hugs, from Aunt Catherine and Uncle Stan. And lots of good wishes and hearty congratulations from Bud and Burly and Uncle Foley, too.

Camilla did not cry. She didn't say much, either, a fact that Joleen hardly noticed, since everyone else seemed to be talking nonstop.

After they'd finished off the pizzas, Joleen said she and Sam had to get on home. Tomorrow, after all, would be a workday. She had laundry to take care of and she needed to fit in a trip to the store. Her refrigerator was empty. In the past few days DeDe's wedding had put her own life completely on hold.

Dekker said he had to get going, too. He walked her to her hatchback economy car before climbing into his battered metal-flake blue Plymouth Road Runner, which he'd had since time began and which bore the dubious distinction of being a year older than he was.

Joleen strapped Sam into his car seat in back and then went around to slide behind the wheel.

Dekker shut her door and leaned in her window. "I thought it went pretty well."

"I thought so, too. But there's a lot more left to tell."

They hadn't even mentioned the change in Dekker's fortunes. That would take some explaining and seemed better accomplished one-on-one. Joleen would tell her mother and Niki the story privately. And she'd tell DeDe, too, as soon as her middle sister returned from her wedding trip.

And then there was the news about the Atwoods. They'd have to get into that unpleasant subject with the family at some point.

And the new baby-sitting arrangements would have to be handled, as well. As a rule DeDe watched Sam in the mornings, Joleen or her mother took over for a couple of hours after lunch. Then when Niki got home from school, she would be on duty until six or so, when Joleen got through at the salon. Dotty Hendershot, the sweet older lady who lived next door to Camilla, in the house where Dekker had grown-up, would pick up the slack.

All that would change now. But further discussion last night had brought them to the conclusion that they didn't have to deal with the child-care issue right away. The wedding would be simple and soon—by the end of the week, they were thinking. And Dekker had proposed a honeymoon, one with Sam included. Dekker said he could afford it, and they both agreed it would be good to have a little time away together, just the three of them, at the start of their new life as a family.

So they would take two weeks for a wedding trip—destination to be decided in the next few days. And when they came home, Joleen would begin looking for the right day care for Sam. By the time the Atwoods geared up to drag her before a judge, she and Dekker would have all the bases covered.

Dekker touched the side of her face. "What is that frown for?"

"Just thinking about how much has to be done."

"Worrying, you mean."

"Maybe…"

"You worry too much, Jo. We'll get to it. To all of it. Little by little."

She produced a smile for him. "I know."

"One thing you do need to deal with right away. Your blood test. I'm going to get mine taken care of tomorrow."

"I've got no appointments between one and three. I'll see if I can fit it in then."

"Good. And what do you think of a week in L.A. and then maybe Maui for the other week?"

"L.A.? Would we visit your brother?"

"If that's okay with you. I have a standing invitation."

"We'd stay at his house?"

"That's right."

"But wouldn't that be inconvenient for him, on such short notice?"

Dekker laughed. "We could stay at Jonas's house for a month and never even set eyes on him, if he didn't want to see us. Angel's Crest is enormous."

"Angel's Crest?"

"The Bravo mansion."

"His house has a *name?*"

"That's right. Angel's Crest is on a hill, in Bel Air. It's an incredible place. Ocean and city views from just about every room in the house. It's been in the Bravo family for three generations, I think Jonas said."

"This is sounding very interesting."

"And did I mention Mandy? I want Sam to meet her."

"Who?"

"Amanda is two. She's Jonas's adopted sister."

"Wait a minute. Your, uh, *real* mother adopted a baby girl, before she died?"

"That's right. And now Jonas and Emma are raising her."

"So Sam will have an aunt who is two?"

"I hadn't thought of it that way, but yes. He will."

"Well, what can I say? Sam just *has* to meet his Aunt Mandy."

"Are you telling me yes to a week in L.A.?"

"I sure am."

"And then Hawaii?"

"Why not?"

"Or maybe I'll just wait. Keep it open-ended. We can decide what we want to do next after we get to L.A."

"That's fine."

"Okay, then." He stepped back from her door, touched his temple in a goodbye salute and headed for his own car.

* * *

Joleen returned to her mother's at eight-thirty the next morning. Camilla had agreed to watch Sam for a couple of hours. Joleen planned to run a few errands without the distractions a toddler presented before she opened the salon at nine-thirty. When she came to work herself, Camilla would take Sam to Dotty next door.

Camilla was never an early riser by choice. Usually, Joleen had to shake her awake and stick a cup of coffee under her nose any time she had baby-sitting duty before ten or so.

But that morning Joleen walked into the kitchen with Sam in her arms and found Camilla sitting in the breakfast nook, her coffee already in front of her, wide-awake and fully dressed.

Joleen started at the sight. "Mama. You're up."

"Yes, I am, baby," said Camilla in a determined tone.

Sam put both hands on Joleen's shoulder and gave a push. "Dow, Mama. Pway."

Joleen bent to let him to the floor. He toddled off toward the living room where Camilla kept a big bin of toys just for him.

"Has Niki already left for school?"

Camilla nodded, picked up her coffee and took a delicate sip.

"Uncle Hubert and everyone finally go home?"

"Yes, they did."

Joleen wondered why it felt as if something wasn't right. "Everything okay, Mama?"

Camilla answered by lifting a shoulder in a shrug.

"Well," Joleen said brightly. "Since you are up

and about, I might as well get goin'. When's your first appointment?''

''I have got a facial and cosmetic consultation at eleven.'' Camilla didn't do hair anymore. She specialized in facial care—everything from herbal masks to makeovers. A couple of years ago she'd brought in a pricey new line of products, which she used and promoted exclusively. The line was a big success, mostly because Camilla had the knack for exploiting and enhancing the natural beauty of each of her clients.

''Okay, then.'' Joleen started for the front door. ''I'll see you at eleven.''

''Baby.'' Her mother's voice was flat.

Joleen turned. ''What *is* the matter, Mama?''

''Have some coffee.''

''I really want to get—''

''I know you do. You *always* do. But whatever it is can wait. We need to talk.''

''Mama, can't we talk a little later? I've got to be at the shop in an hour and before that I want to—''

''Don't argue with me, now. Get yourself some coffee and sit down here with me.''

''Mama, I have got to get goin'.''

Her mother just looked at her.

''Oh, all right.'' Joleen got a mug from the cupboard, filled it and took the chair across from her mother. ''Now, what is it that just cannot wait?''

Camilla had stopped looking at Joleen. Now she stared into her coffee cup, her mouth drawn down at the corners, as if there might be something in there that shouldn't be.

Joleen, who needed to get to the cleaners and make

a quick stop at WalMart before she headed over to one of the major beauty supply houses to pick up a few popular products they had run low on, couldn't keep herself from making a small, impatient sound in her throat.

Camilla heaved a deep sigh and shook her head at her coffee cup. "I find I don't quite know how to say this."

That suits me just fine, Joleen thought. "It's okay. We can talk later." She started to stand. "Tonight, after—"

"No, you don't." Camilla's hand closed over her arm. "You are not escapin' me."

Joleen stared at her mother's hand, which was soft and slim, the smooth square-filed nails polished a shimmery bronze. It did not look like the hand of a fifty-year-old woman, not by a long shot. Joleen wished her own hands looked half that good. But Joleen still did hair. And she had no shampoo girl, so she spent a lot of her working life knuckle-deep in lather. Very hard on the hands.

Camilla said. "I have been awake half the night worryin' over you."

"Why?"

"Sit back down."

Joleen dropped into the chair again. "All right, Mama. I'm sitting. Talk."

"I am just going to ask you directly."

"I sure wish you would."

Camilla let go of Joleen's arm and threw up both hands. "What on God's green earth has possessed you to think a marriage between you and Dekker is a good idea?"

Joleen felt pure indignation. She decided to let it show. "Mama! I *love* Dekker. And he loves me."

Camilla smacked one slim, soft hand on the table and waved the other one in the air. "Yes, and I love your uncle Foley. But I never would marry him."

"Uncle Foley is your *brother,* Mama."

"Exactly. And that's how I love him. Like a brother. The same way that you love Dekker Smith."

Oh, this was getting sticky already. As Joleen had known it would, as she'd tried to get Dekker to understand it would.

Half-truths and evasions, she though glumly. Comin' right up...

"Well?" said her mother on a hard huff of breath.

"I love him," Joleen said again, and she stared her mother straight in the eye.

Her mother stared right back. "You don't love him the way a woman loves a man," she accused. "And he doesn't have that soul feelin' for you, either."

"You do not know that," Joleen said. "You do not know what we feel."

"Oh, yes I do. I know my baby. And I know Lorraine's boy. I also know that you both deserve better than to marry a person who does not set your heart on fire. You both deserve it all. Passion and excitement. And magic. I want those things for you—and I want them for Dekker, too."

Joleen wrapped her hands around her cup. The warmth felt comforting against her palms. She said honestly, "Both Dekker and I had those things once, Mama. They didn't last."

"Bobby Atwood and Stacey?" Her mother made a low, scoffing sound.

Joleen's indignation level rose again. "Yes. Bobby Atwood. And Stacey. You know how Dekker was about Stacey."

"There *were* terrible problems in that marriage, baby."

"I know that. I am not saying they didn't have problems. I am only saying he loved her. In a passionate way. A *soul* way. And Bobby, well, it shames me to have to admit it now, but I was long gone in love with that man."

"Oh, that is *so* not true."

"Mama—"

"You *thought* you were long gone in love with that man. You *wanted* to be. You were waiting for your knight in shinin' armor to thunder in on a fine white horse and sweep you away. You waited a long time. When that young Atwood showed up, with his smooth talk and his fancy car and winnin' smile, you were like a nice, ripe peach, just ready to drop off the tree. And you did drop. You dropped good and hard. But that was not—"

"Mama—"

"Pardon me. I believe that I was still speaking."

"Fine. Speak. Finish."

"What I'm saying is—and you *are* listening, aren't you?"

Joleen gritted her teeth. "I am, Mama. I am listening."

Camilla's eyebrows had a skeptical lift—but she did continue. "What I'm saying is that what happened with Bobby Atwood was not it—was not love. And Dekker and Stacey, well, that was certainly *something*, but it wasn't *it*, either. Not the real, true, deep lifelong passion I am talking about. Not what I had with your daddy. Not what DeDe has with Wayne.''

"Mama. Some people never find that kind of love.''

"We are not talking about some people. We are talking about you. And Dekker. My first baby. And my best friend's little boy.''

"Well, maybe you have to stop thinking of us that way—as your baby and Lorraine's little boy. We are grown people now. We have a right to make our own decisions about life. And about who we will love.''

"I never said that you didn't. I just don't like this.'' Camilla looked into her cup again—and then sharply up to snare her daughter's gaze. "Something else is goin' on here. I know it. I can feel it.''

Joleen kept her face composed—and told some more lies. "Nothing is going on, Mama. I don't know what you mean.''

"Oh, you do. You know. There is something....'' Camilla pushed her cup to the side and leaned across the table. "Is it...those Atwood people? You went off alone with them, didn't you, before they left the wedding Saturday? I saw you go inside with them.''

Joleen opened her mouth to let out more lies. And then shut it. Camilla would have to hear the truth about the Atwoods sooner or later.

"Yes,'' Joleen said. "They wanted to talk to me.''

"About...?''

Sam was too quiet. Joleen stood.

"What is it now?'' muttered her mother. But Camilla had had three children of her own. She nodded. "Go on. Check—and then get right back in here.''

Joleen went through the dining room. She found her little boy sitting on the hooked rug near the big window at the front of the house, playing with the wooden blocks one of the uncles had given him for his first birthday six months before.

Sam looked up. "How," he said, beaming proudly at the crooked stacks of blocks in front of him.

"Yes," said Joleen, her chest suddenly tight. "A very fine house." She would do anything—*anything,* including telling her dear mama a thousand rotten lies—to keep her boy safe, to be there whenever he needed her. To get to see his face now and then when he smiled like he was smiling now....

She took in a deep breath to loosen those bands of emotion that had squeezed around her heart. Then she asked slowly, pronouncing each word with care, "Come in the kitchen? With Grandma and me?"

He shook his head and loosed a string of nonsense syllables.

"You mean, you want to stay here?"

"Pway."

She wanted to scoop him up hard against her heart, to hug him until he squirmed to get down. But no. He was content, sitting on her mama's rug, playing with his house of blocks. Why ruin that?

"Okay. Be good."

"I goo."

Her steps dragging, Joleen returned to the breakfast nook. She slid back into her chair. "He's fine."

"All right. What did the Atwoods want to talk with you about?"

Joleen took a fortifying sip of her coffee. And then she told her mother everything that had transpired in her father's study before the Atwoods took their leave.

When she had finished, Camilla picked up her coffee cup, started to sip, realized it was empty and set it back down—hard. "Oh sweetheart, the nerve of those people."

"I hear you, Mama."

"I did not like that Robert Atwood. Right from the first I saw that he would be trouble. Thinks he's a cut above, doesn't he? That he's better than the rest of us. And the woman, Antonia? Well, I'm willin' to admit I felt sorry for her. Scared of her own shadow, and wearing *mauve,* of all colors. Much too cool for her. Just faded her right out to nothin' at all. She needs a bright, warm palette, to bring out that peach tone in her."

"Mama."

"Oh, well, all right. I'm rambling and I know it. It's just, what else can I say, but how dare they?"

"I asked myself that same question."

Camilla folded those beautiful hands on the table-top. "I think I am starting to understand it all now. You and Dekker have been scheming. You've decided that the two of you getting married is somehow going to help you keep the Atwoods from stealin' our Sam."

Joleen gulped. "No, Mama. Of course not. You asked me what happened with them, and I told you. It's got nothin' to do with Dekker and me."

"Oh, sweetheart. You are such a bad liar. You shouldn't even try it."

Joleen only wanted to get out of there. "I am marrying Dekker, Mama. That is all there is to it."

"But you don't *love* him—not the way you need to love the man you bind your life with."

Joleen stood. "I am saying this once more. I want you to listen. I do love Dekker. And Dekker loves me.

We are getting married as soon as possible, and we are going to be happy. You just wait and see.''

"But you don't—''

"Mama. Enough. You have said your piece, and I have heard it. This decision, though, is mine to make.''

Camilla was shaking her head, her mouth all pursed up, brow furrowed. At that moment she looked her age—and more. She said, very softly and with heavy regret, "I know I was never the mother I should have been.''

Joleen glared down at her. "You are *my* mother. If I was startin' all over, and God gave me a chance to choose, you are the one I would pick in an instant.''

"Oh, baby…''

"Do not start in cryin' on me, Mama. I just don't have the time or the patience for that right now.''

"I only…I wanted so much *more* for you.''

"Well, this is about what *I* want. And I want to marry Dekker. I want to make a life with him.'' It surprised her, how firm she sounded. How secure in her choice.

On the counter, the coffeemaker made a gurgling sound, and somewhere outside, a leaf blower started up.

Camilla's tears spilled over, they trailed down her soft cheeks. "Well, I have told you my feelings on this.''

Joleen held her ground. "And I have said what I will do.''

There was a box of tissues, ready and waiting, in the center of the table. Her mother yanked one out. "I love you, baby.''

"And I love you, Mama.''

"And no mistake—" Camilla had to pause, to blow her nose. Then she started again. "No mistake is so big that love can't find a way to make it right in the end."

Chapter Seven

Joleen fitted in her blood test later that day. The lab said she would have her results by Thursday. That night she and Dekker decided they would marry on Friday afternoon at the Oklahoma County Courthouse.

Joleen called DeDe in Mississippi.

"Oh, I cannot stand it," DeDe wailed when Joleen shared the news. "You are my sister and Dekker is the only brother I have ever known and if you two are getting married on Friday, Wayne and I are comin' home right now."

Dekker got on the line with her and managed to calm her down. He told her they would miss her, but on no account would he allow her to cut her honeymoon short. He finally got her to promise to stay in Mississippi for another week as planned.

Camilla, Niki and Sam would attend the short ceremony. As for the rest of the family, Joleen told them that she loved them all dearly, but she and Dekker could only have so many guests at the courthouse.

"Well then, do not have it at the courthouse, hon," argued Aunt LeeAnne.

Joleen explained that she wasn't quite up for planning another big wedding so soon after the one she'd put together for her sister. She said that she and Dekker just wanted to get the formalities over with and start living their lives side by side.

They all said they understood. But they didn't. Joleen could see it in their eyes.

"We *have* to do *something*," Aunt LeeAnne insisted. "Just a little family get-together when you come home from the courthouse. At least we can have that."

So it was agreed. After the civil ceremony, the cousins and uncles and aunts would be waiting at Camilla's. They would have chips and dips and little sandwiches with the crusts cut off. They'd bring a few wedding gifts and they'd offer their heartfelt congratulations.

At the courthouse both Niki and Camilla cried a lot. Camilla had no reservations about explaining to Joleen why she was crying.

"Because another of my babies is saying 'I do.' Because I know there is more goin' on here than I have been told about. Because, well, I do feel that I have been cheated of giving you the kind of wedding DeDe had, a real *family* wedding, which you know I believe every woman deserves…and because I wish my best friend could be here on this day of all days— but I know, if Lorraine *were* back with us again, she'd just be headin' off to jail. And that plain breaks my heart.''

By then the whole family had learned the truth about Dekker's real identity.

And they hadn't found out quite the way Joleen and Dekker had intended.

Dekker had left his apartment Tuesday morning to find five reporters lurking outside. They all wanted to interview him, to get the first statements from the long-lost Bravo Baby. Dekker told them to get lost.

He got a call from his brother an hour or so after he chased the reporters away. Jonas told him that the story had broken in Los Angeles that morning. He urged Dekker not to let it bother him. He said it had been bound to leak out sooner or later.

"As a Bravo," Jonas warned. "You'll have to get used to being in the spotlight now and then."

"No, I won't," said Dekker.

Jonas laughed and assured Dekker that the whole thing would blow over eventually.

By Wednesday the wire services had gotten hold of it. The tale of how Dekker Smith was really Russell Bravo of the fabulously wealthy southern California Bravos made the second page of the *Daily Oklahoman*. And everyone in the family had been able to read all about it for themselves.

So part of the reason that Camilla cried through Joleen's wedding was because she had recently learned that her best friend in the whole world had not been Dekker's mama, after all, but the accomplice of the evil uncle who had stolen him from his *real* mother—

who, as it turned out, had died just a few short months ago, never having seen her precious second son again.

Niki cried for her own reasons. Because her big sister and her beloved Dek were getting married, and because her mother was crying, and because…well, just because.

Dekker had found the time to go out and buy Joleen a ring. It was so beautiful—two curving rows of diamonds set into the band, surrounding a single large marquise-cut stone. He kissed her after the judge pronounced them man and wife—a light kiss, hardly more than a gentle brushing of his mouth across her own.

Right then her mother and sister burst into renewed sobbing. Joleen and Dekker turned from each other to try to settle them down.

They all went back to Camilla's house together, in the beautiful new silver-gray Lexus that Dekker had bought the day before. Two cars filled with reporters followed along behind.

"Ignore them," commanded Dekker, his voice a low growl.

Joleen granted him her most unconcerned smile. "No problem." And it wasn't. For her. She was a little worried about her new husband, though. Since Tuesday, news people seemed to be popping up wherever Dekker went. He was getting very tired of it.

"You go on in," he said when they got to her mother's. "Give me a minute."

Joleen put her hand on his sleeve. "What are you going to do?"

"Have a few words with the media."

"What will you say?"

"That I'd appreciate a little privacy on my wedding day."

"Don't you think that it might be better if—"

"Jo. Go in. I won't be long."

She could tell by the thrust of that cleft chin of his that it would get her nowhere to keep after him, so she got her son from his car seat and herded her mother and sister toward the front door.

The aunts and uncles and cousins and lots of finger foods were waiting inside. Joleen moved from one set of loving arms to the next, getting kissed and congratulated by one and all.

"Well, don't you look beautiful," said Aunt LeeAnne, stepping back to admire Joleen's ivory-colored street-length silk sheath and the short, fitted jacket that went with it.

Joleen thanked her aunt and kept an eye on the front door until Dekker slipped through it a few minutes later.

"How did it go out there?" she asked him, when she finally got him aside for a moment.

He shrugged. "They said they would leave."

"They're gone, then?"

"I have my doubts. They all have this kind of glassy-eyed, hungry stare when they deal with me. To them, I'm not even really human. I'm just a story they'll do anything to get. Maybe I should have listened to you and left it alone—and don't give me that I-told-you-so look."

"I'm sure I do not know what look you are talkin' about."

"The one on your face right now."

She made a show of crossing her eyes—and then

grew more serious. "Did you tell them straight out that we just got married?"

"Hell, yes. They followed us from the courthouse, and that leads me to believe they probably already knew—which is just fine. Let Robert Atwood read all about how you've married the famous—and rich— Bravo Baby, let him think about the ways it will mess up his plans. Let him—"

"Hey, you two," called Uncle Hubert from over by the big bowl of sparkling-wine punch that Aunt Catherine had made. "Stop that whispering. Get over here with the rest of us. Time for a little toast…"

"Yes, come over here right now." Camilla paused to sob and dab at her eyes with a tissue. "We want to wish you both the best of everything."

Camilla cried until six-thirty. But then the doorbell rang. It was one of Wayne's bachelor uncles from the wedding the week before—the one who had stayed so late last Saturday night. The uncle, whose name was Ezra Clay, did not come empty-handed. He had a gift for the newlyweds and a huge bouquet of tiger lilies for the mother of the bride.

At the sight of her admirer, Camilla ran upstairs to freshen her makeup. When she came back down, she took Ezra Clay's hand and led him to the kitchen. They stayed in there for quite a while. When Joleen went in to hunt down more pretzels, her mother and Wayne's uncle were standing close together at the counter, a tall crystal vase in front of them. Half the lilies stood in the vase, half lay in wait, bright splashes of sable-spotted gold, on the counter.

Camilla chose a flower from those waiting on the

counter, clipped the stem at an angle with her gardening shears, and carefully propped it up in the vase. Then she leaned close to Wayne's uncle and whispered something.

The uncle laughed, a low, intimate sound. Camilla laughed, too, and leaned close again to whisper some more.

Joleen watched them from the corner of her eye as she got a fresh bag of pretzels from the cupboard by the stove. Ezra Clay could have been anywhere from forty-five to sixty. He had intelligent dark eyes and nice, broad shoulders. He owned a couple of ice-cream store franchises, Joleen thought she remembered Wayne mentioning once.

Could this be the man who would convince her mother to settle down at last?

Sure. And maybe tomorrow the sun would set in the east.

Joleen closed the cupboard door. Whether Ezra Clay lasted in her mother's affections or not, Joleen was grateful to him. Camilla had not shed a single tear since he'd walked in the front door.

Romance, Joleen thought wryly, did have its uses.

Dekker, Joleen and Sam left the party at a little after nine. The reporters—who had *not* gone away when Dekker asked them to—snapped pictures when the newlyweds emerged from the house, their flashes explosions of blinding light in the warm autumn darkness. Then they jumped into their cars, ready to give chase.

Dekker swore under his breath as he swung out of

Camilla's driveway. "They said they'd leave us alone for tonight, damn it."

"Well, they are not doing it." Joleen fastened her seat belt. "Take your own advice and ignore them."

Dekker muttered a few swear words under his breath. Joleen pretended not to hear. She smiled and waved at the family members who had gathered on the porch to watch them drive away.

"And how the hell am I supposed to see to drive?" Dekker grumbled as they took off down the street. He had to squint through the words Just Married, which Bud and Burly had scrawled on the windshield in shaving cream. There Goes the Bride was written on the rear window. And a bouncing row of tin cans clattered along behind them.

Joleen brushed the birdseed from her hair. "It's three blocks to my place. Take it slow and we'll make it okay." They'd chosen to stay at Joleen's house for the wedding night. First thing in the morning they were leaving for Los Angeles.

As soon as they turned the corner and all the waving relatives disappeared from sight, Dekker swung over and stopped at the curb.

"What now?" Joleen demanded, as one of the reporters' cars slid in behind them and the other rolled past the Lexus and nosed in along the curb just ahead.

Dekker whipped out his Swiss Army knife—the one with three blades, a corkscrew and just about every other tool known to man tucked inside. "Be right back."

"Dekker—"

He was out of the car before she could tell him to stay where he was. She watched him circle around to the rear bumper, where he crouched, disappearing from her line of sight. When he stood again, he had the cans, still hanging by their strings.

He came back to the front of the car and presented them to her. "Here. Do something with these."

Like what? she thought, but decided not to ask. She took them and set them on the floor next to her door. They rattled together as Dekker swung away from the curb. He passed the car in front before the reporter at the wheel had the wherewithal to shift into drive.

"I thought you said you couldn't see," Joleen reminded him as the powerful car picked up speed.

"I'm managing."

"Lord, I hope so."

"And this baby handles like a dream."

"Oh. Good news to all of us, I am sure...."

Sam laughed in pure glee from the back seat. He let out a string of almost-words, followed by a rousing, "Vroom-vroom-vroom!"

Joleen clutched the armrest and thought of all the times she'd suggested her friend ought to get himself a new car. And now he had done it. She could almost wish he hadn't.

But then again, his old Road Runner, which still sat beneath the carport outside his apartment building, boasted 383 cubes on a V-8 block—a fact he mentioned often and with considerable pride. If he'd been driving it right now, they'd be going at the same speeds—and the ride would have been a whole lot rougher.

They barreled around a corner, tin cans rolling at her feet. "Dekker..."

He wasn't listening. "Very fine," he murmured, "like a knife through warm butter..."

In seconds they reached another corner and spun around it. Joleen shoved the cans out of the way, braced her feet more firmly and told herself she ought to be grateful he hadn't bought that Ferrari he'd mentioned Wednesday.

"Maybe later," he'd decided, after considering the Ferrari. "First, I want to get us a nice family car."

The Lexus was a four-door. In Dekker's mind, that made it a family car, though clearly, what it had under the hood would stack up against that old Road Runner of his any day of the week.

They took two more corners at speeds faster than Joleen wanted to think about. Then at last Dekker applied the brakes. "Well?" he asked.

She glanced behind them. The dark street was deserted. "You lost them."

"Vroom-vroom-vroom," said Sam.

Dekker readjusted his rearview mirror. "You haven't seen any of them hanging around your place, right?"

"No, I have not."

"Good. Then maybe they haven't figured out where you live yet. Which means we'll be left alone tonight. And tomorrow, we are outta here."

"I cannot wait." She gave him a look, one that told him just what she thought of his driving so fast.

He grinned back at her, not sorry in the least.

Dekker drove around—at a sedate speed—for another fifteen minutes. "Just to make certain I shook those fools."

The dashboard clock said it was 9:33 when he

pulled up in front of the tidy one-story house that Joleen had been calling home for a little over a year.

"We'd better hide this car," he said. "If our
'friends' decide to cruise the neighborhood, it would
be a dead giveaway."

So Joleen got out and moved her own car from the
small detached garage at the side of the house. Once
Dekker had parked in the vacant space, she went to
get Sammy. "And put those tin cans in the recycling
bin," she said as she leaned in the car to free her son
from his safety seat.

Dekker, who stood behind her at that point, made a
put-upon sound in his throat and muttered, "What?
You? Anal?"

She pulled her head out of the car just long enough
to make a face at him before she reached back in to
scoop Sammy out of the seat and into her arms.

Joleen's house was very much like a lot of the
smaller houses in Mesta Park. A classic prairie cottage,
it had no hallways. Living room, dining room and
kitchen opened into each other, a bedroom off each.
The single bath was tucked between the two back bedrooms.

Joleen had the room off the kitchen and Sam had
the one in the middle. The largest bedroom, in front,
with a nice window facing the porch but without direct
access to the bath, served as her guest room. Dekker
carried his overnight bag in there as Joleen took her
son with her into her own room. She swiftly changed
out of her wedding dress and into a pair of capris and
a crop top.

Then Sammy had his bath. He went right down

when she put him to bed, turning his face toward the wall and sighing in tired contentment. Joleen tiptoed from the room, switching off the light and pulling the door quietly closed behind her.

She found Dekker sitting in the kitchen, his back to the window, at the old pine table she'd picked up at a yard sale and refinished herself. He'd changed clothes, too. Now he wore faded jeans and an OSU T-shirt.

She tipped her head at the open Rolling Rock in front of him. "I see you managed to find the beer."

He picked up the bottle and toasted her with it— then set it down without drinking from it. "What a damn day."

"You said it." She got herself a Coke from the fridge and dropped into the chair across from him. "At least Uncle Hubert didn't get falling-down drunk."

"That's true. We need to be grateful for small favors. But I have a request."

"Name it."

"Can we stop having weddings for a while?"

She raised her right hand, palm out. "I do solemnly swear. If there is another weddin' in the next five years, we will not have a thing to do with it."

He leaned back in the chair, crossed his feet in front of him and tipped his beer at her again. "But what if it's Callie's?"

"Callie is on her own."

"You think I believe that? If Callie and that cowboy tie the knot, you'll be planning the menu and helping her pick out her long white dress."

"Think what you want."

"And what about Niki?"

"What about her?"

"What if she decides to get married?"

"My baby sister is thirteen. I will not *allow* her to get married in the next five years."

"Maybe Camilla—"

"Dekker. *Please*."

"I think she likes the ice cream man. A lot."

"She likes them *all* a lot. But they never do last, and you know that as well as I do."

"Who's the cynical one now?"

"I'm not bein'—" She cut herself off. Something had happened in his face, though his body remained just as before, slouched in the chair, totally relaxed.

"Don't tense up," he said low. "Pretend nothing has changed."

"Well, all right." She sat back herself, crossed her own ankles and drank from her Coke.

He winked at her. "You're a champion."

"Thank you. And what, by the way, is going on?"

"Keep your eyes on me."

"Okay..."

"I heard something. I think there's someone outside the window behind me—and don't shift your focus there."

"You mean—?"

"Reporters. It looks like they've found us, after all. But don't say it—don't say anything about it. Whoever's out there won't be able to hear much through the window, but the view of your face through those lace curtains should be pretty good, considering that the overhead light is on and the shades are up."

She understood. Whoever it was might be able to

make out her words as her lips moved—though why it should matter, she wasn't quite sure.

Dekker said, "I want to give our uninvited guest a little taste of his own medicine. And do not start frowning. Please."

She put on a big smile.

"Don't overplay it."

She toned it down.

He shifted forward, drawing his legs up and resting his forearms on the table. "Lean toward me."

Still grinning—but not too hard—she mimicked his pose, which brought their noses within inches of each other. "Now what?"

"Now, I want you to kiss me."

Joleen almost blinked—but stopped herself in time.

"Just do it," Dekker whispered.

"But—"

"Humor me."

"What good is—"

"Jo."

That was all he said. Her name. It was enough to remind her of the trust she put in him, of what a true friend he was and always had been.

She would jump off a cliff for him if he asked her to. What was a kiss compared to that?

She leaned even closer.

And their lips met.

His lips were soft. Warm. She wondered if hers felt cool to him. And then she thought of their brief kiss at the courthouse.

This made it two times.

Two times in her whole life that she had kissed

Dekker's mouth—and both of those times were on the same day, their *wedding* day.

His mouth moved against hers. "Close your eyes."

It was a most ticklish feeling, talking together, with their lips touching. She couldn't help smiling. "Dekker, I know how to kiss."

"Do you?"

"Yes, I do."

"Well, okay then. Prove it."

Joleen rose to the challenge, letting her mouth go soft and her eyelids drift down.

Several seconds passed. Very lovely seconds.

Dekker's mouth opened slightly against hers. She felt the warm flick of his tongue.

It was…shocking.

Dekker's tongue. Touching the moistness just inside her lips.

Shocking.

But not the least bit unpleasant.

Some part of her mind rebelled. This, after all, wasn't what the two of them were about. Not Joleen and Dekker. Brushing kisses—quick, fond pecks on the cheek—those were all right. But nothing mouth-to-mouth. Nothing involving wetness. Nothing including tongues.

However…

Somebody ought to teach those reporters a lesson. And this would do it—though she wasn't quite sure how.

But Dekker knew. And that was good enough for her.

She sighed.

He made a low, teasing sound in his throat and went

on kissing her. With tenderness. And considerable skill.

Not deeply, though. He never did more than skim the secret flesh right inside her mouth.

Not deeply...

A memory flared, bright as those photoflashes on her mama's front porch earlier that night.

Herself at the age of eleven. Spying on a sixteen-year-old Dekker, who was with Lucy Doherty, his first serious girlfriend.

They were kissing, Dekker and Lucy. Sitting on that little iron bench in the corner of Lorraine's backyard, kissing long and deep and slow. Joleen, behind the fence next door, could see them through the space between the fence boards.

So strange. All these years later. Here she was, her mouth against Dekker's mouth. Thinking of him kissing Lucy Doherty, of her own naughty young self, with her snoopy little nose pressed to the fence.

The way he'd kissed Lucy, now *that* had been a deep kiss.

Joleen was starting to wonder what it might feel like if Dekker were to kiss *her* deeply when she realized he was pulling away.

She sighed for the second time and let her lashes drift open.

His blue, blue eyes gleamed at her. "Good job."

"I aim to please." The words came out as a throaty purr. Did she intend them to? She wasn't sure. "Um, what now?"

"Now, we get up from this table and we go into your bedroom with our arms around each other. We

want it to look as if, when we get in there, we're going
to do what newlyweds usually do.''

What newlyweds usually do…

The words set her pulse throbbing. Which was so
silly. They were not *really* going to do what newlyweds do.

They were only going to make the reporter think
that they would.

Why are we doing this, really? she wanted to ask.
But she didn't quite dare. She still faced the window,
and the light overhead seemed way too bright, too re-
vealing. Whoever was out there might know what she
said. That would ruin Dekker's plan—whatever his
plan was, which she didn't know yet.

She didn't want that, to ruin her friend's plan—her
friend who, as of tonight, was her husband, too….

But then, not *really* her husband. At least, not in
that way.

''Ready?'' he asked.

She swallowed. Nodded.

He held out his hand to her.

She laid hers in it—her left hand, the one on which
she now wore the shining band of diamonds he'd
given her at the courthouse. Holding on, he rose and
came around to her side of the table, his eyes locked
with hers the whole time.

He pulled her out of the chair and wrapped an arm
around her, tucking her in close to the side of his big,
hard body. It was six steps to her bedroom door. He
flipped the wall switch as they passed it. The kitchen
went dark. He drew her over the threshold, kicking the
door shut behind them.

She started to reach for the light switch, but he

caught her hand. "No. Not the overhead light..." His breath teased her ear.

He left her, a shadow moving on silent feet, drawing the shades. Since her room was at a back corner of the house, there were two windows, one on the left wall next to the bed and one to the right of the headboard.

She remained at the door, waiting.

"And now?" she whispered, when both shades were lowered.

She heard a click as he switched on her bedside lamp. In its soft glow, he returned to her, took her shoulders in a gentle grip.

She frowned up into his shadowed face. "Dekker, what—?"

"Wait here. By the door. Don't get in front of the lamp. The light should draw him, but he shouldn't be able to see anything, really."

"But what are you going to *do?*"

Again, he refused to answer. "Wait here. I won't be long."

"But—"

He touched her mouth for silence. "Just wait."

She rolled her eyes at him and shrugged.

"Is that a yes?"

So she gave him the nod he seemed to require.

He went out through the other door—the one that led to the bathroom and Sammy's room and from there, to the dining room.

Joleen slid to the floor. She wrapped her arms around her drawn-up legs and propped her chin on her knees.

Great. Now she got to wait, while Dekker played detective.

And what was the *point,* she wanted to know?

He'd already asked those news people to leave. It hadn't worked. He'd tried ditching them. Without success.

What else could he do?

She realized what and started to stand again.

But no.

She sank back down. She had told him she would wait here. Okay, she would wait.

And if he got himself into a fight tonight, he'd better be prepared to hear a few harsh words from her later. Because she would be sharing with him a large piece of her mind.

Dekker pushed open the door to Sam's room and froze, listening.

Once he heard the shallow, even breathing that told him Sam was fast asleep, he moved forward. He stopped at the door to the dining room. The faint sliver of brightness beneath it confirmed what he remembered; there was a light on in the front of the house, the floor lamp Joleen had switched on low when they first came in the front door. Other than that—and the lamp in Jo's room—the house was dark.

Good.

Dekker opened the door and slid through it, pulling it silently closed behind him. Keeping near the wall, he went beneath the arch into the front room, where that single lamp burned. He'd left the guest room door ajar. He ducked through it.

The shades were up in there. Dekker flattened himself against the wall by the window that opened onto the front porch. He waited.

Nothing. No sounds or movements beyond the window. He hoped that meant the porch was deserted, that the damn reporter was on the prowl around back, trying to get a look in Joleen's bedroom window, to steal a shot of the famous Bravo Baby making love to his bride.

The window creaked a little as Dekker slid it up. He slipped back into the shadows, waited some more. He heard only innocent noises: a horn honking a block or so away; wind chimes on the porch next door; the intermittent bark of a lonely dog in the distance.

Dekker counted to three hundred. Slowly. Then he moved into the window again, to unhook the screen. It swung out. He held it clear and went through.

The porch provided no surprises. Keeping as much in the shadows as possible, Dekker moved down to the opposite end, by the front room, and slid over the rail to the ground. The night was clear, bright with stars. The waning moon rode high, and there wasn't much cover on that side of the house. But he was in luck. No reporters lurked there.

Maybe they'd given up and gone away.

Or maybe they had moved around to the back of the house where he had hoped to lure them.

Swiftly and silently he covered the distance from the front porch to the back. He pressed himself to the wall at the end of the house and stole a look around the corner.

Yes.

The soft glow from the lamp in Jo's room showed him a figure—male—in dark pants and shirt, perched on the side rail of her small back porch, craning to see through the narrow slit between the blind and the window frame.

Perfect, thought Dekker. Off balance, with his back to me.

He slid around the corner and made for the porch steps.

His target barely had time to turn and grunt, "Huh?" before Dekker grabbed his arm, twisted it up behind him and yanked him down from the rail and hard back against his own body, keeping the arm up at an unnatural angle—and getting a nice, tight lock around the neck.

The camera around that neck swung as Dekker's captive struggled.

"Easy," Dekker whispered. "I'm not going to hurt you. We're just going to have a nice little talk."

The body in his grip stopped fighting him. "Whatever you say…"

Dekker knew that voice. He murmured a low oath. "Pollard."

"Got me."

"I thought you were a reporter."

"'Fraid not."

"What the hell are you doing here?"

"Man's gotta make a living, Smith."

Dekker gave his captive's arm a slight upward push. Pollard let out a sharp grunt of pain. Dekker whispered, "Who are you working for?" As if he didn't already know.

"Look. Could you ease off on the arm a little?"

"I want some answers."

"You'll get them. Just back the hell off."

Chapter Eight

Joleen heard a thud on the back porch. And then faint scuffling sounds, followed by the mutter of low voices.

Dekker had found his man.

She listened for the heavy thumps and pained grunts that would have indicated a brawl in progress. She simply was not going to put up with any brawl on her back porch.

But no such noises occurred. So she kept her word and waited there on the floor of her bedroom, her back against the kitchen door, her knees drawn up to her chest.

Dekker returned to her the way he had left. He appeared in the doorway to the bathroom.

She gave a push with her feet and slid upright. "Well?"

He pulled the door closed behind him. "For the

moment our visitor is gone. Too bad we all know he won't stay that way.'' Dekker held out his hand. ''I confiscated these.'' Three rolls of film sat in his palm.

Joleen stared at the rolls and thought about the long, sweet, not-deep-enough kiss she and Dekker had shared at her kitchen table—the kiss, she reminded herself, that had been purely for the reporter's benefit. She wondered how many shots the man had taken through the kitchen window. Not that it mattered now, since Dekker had the film.

Dekker turned from her. He broke open the rolls and dropped the ruined film into the wastebasket by the closet door.

Joleen went to the bed and sat on the edge. ''I can see what you mean, about those reporters.'' She flopped onto her back with a sigh. ''They get old real fast.''

Dekker was silent.

She lifted her head off the bed and frowned at him. ''What?''

''That was no reporter, Jo.''

She hauled herself to a sitting position again. ''Then what?''

''P.I.,'' he said flatly. ''Name's Pollard. Dickson Pollard. Used to be on the OCPD. Now, he's on the payroll at Ace Security, the biggest—and some say the best—agency in the city.''

Joleen felt her skin crawl. ''Robert Atwood.'' Righteous indignation burned along her every nerve. ''Robert Atwood hired him to spy on me.''

''Jo. It's not exactly a big surprise.''

''That man has probably been takin' pictures of me

for weeks, hasn't he? Peeking in my windows, spying on my life.''

''Look at it this way. The situation hasn't changed. You just know for sure now, that's all.''

She scowled at her friend. ''Why doesn't that make me feel any better?''

He came and dropped down beside her on the bed. ''Because it's a violation of your privacy, of your right to lead your life without people who mean less than nothing to you—total strangers—poking their damn noses in it.'' There was heat in his voice.

She found her own anger had worn itself out. Weariness took its place. She leaned her head on his shoulder. ''I think now I understand a little better how you've felt the last few days, with all those reporters following you everywhere you go. It's not fun.''

''No. It is not.''

''And I guess, even though you took his film, that detective will still be reporting what he saw to Robert Atwood.''

Dekker made a low noise of agreement. ''No way to stop him—short of keeping him captive or murdering him.''

''But that's good, right? Robert Atwood will read in the papers that we are married. And Dickson Pollard will report that he saw us acting like newlyweds.''

''Exactly.''

They sat for a moment without speaking.

Finally, Dekker muttered, ''I'll bet you're beat. We should go to bed.'' He started to stand.

She realized she didn't want him to go.

And, now she thought about it, he probably *shouldn't* go.

She grabbed his hand before he could get away from her. "Dekker..." He let her pull him back down beside her. "It just occurred to me. Maybe you ought to sleep in here—I mean, in case that Pollard guy comes back. If you're sleepin' in the guest room, won't that cause suspicion, about the two of us, about whether our marriage is the real thing or not?"

"I'll keep the light off and the shades down. You do the same. If Pollard does come back tonight, he won't have a clue where either of us is sleeping."

That made perfect sense. She felt foolish, suddenly, for suggesting otherwise. She just knew her face was cherry red.

"And after tonight," he added, blessedly oblivious to her embarrassment, "for two weeks, we won't be here to spy on. When we get back we'll find a new house. I'll make sure security there is state-of-the-art."

She forgot all about her red face. "We're going to move?" Joleen loved her little house. Her uncle Stan, who made his living buying rundown houses, repairing them, and then selling them again, had found it for her. Uncle Stan had also made sure she got a great price and small mortgage payments. She'd put in a lot of time and tender loving care to fix it up just the way she wanted it. "We didn't talk about moving."

"No, but we will have to move."

"*Have* to?"

He lifted an eyebrow at her. "You have a problem with moving?"

"I, well, I suppose I thought that you could just..." She let the sentence trail off.

He finished it for her. "Move in here?"

"Is that so impossible?"

"Come on, Jo. You've got one bathroom—accessible only through your bedroom and Sam's."

"We could add another bath."

"Why not buy a bigger house, something more suited to the three of us? We can afford it. We can afford any damn house we want."

"But…" she began, then didn't really know how to go on. What he said did make sense.

"Jo." He was shaking his head at her. His eyes looked so soft. "I know you love your house. But there are going to be changes. You have to accept that."

She folded her hands in her lap and stared down at them. "You're right. And I…I want us both to be happy with this marriage of ours." She raised her head, gave him a smile. "We should live in a house we've chosen together."

Now his expression was the next thing to tender. "Did I ever tell you I like your attitude?"

"Some call me anal. Can you believe that?"

"Never." He cupped the back of her head in his big hand and pressed his lips to her forehead. When he pulled away and met her eyes again, she could still feel that kiss on her skin, a sensation of sweet warmth and gentle pressure.

He stood. "So who gets the bathroom first?"

"Be my guest."

"I'll be three minutes…max."

"No hurry."

"I'll just go in and out through Sam's room."

Awkward, she thought. This is awkward, the two of us, married but *not* married. Will it always be this way?

No, she told herself. Of course not. They would grow accustomed to living in the same house, to each other's day-to-day ways. They'd be like roommates, eventually. Roommates, only better. Because of the bond that had made them family to each other long before their marriage. Because they were the dearest of friends.

And their moving would ease the awkwardness, too. With a bigger house they could each have a lot more privacy.

"Jo?" He was staring down at her, waiting for her to answer him.

What was the question? "Oh. Sorry. Go ahead. Through Sam's room." He turned to leave her—and she stopped him before he could open the bathroom door. "Dekker."

He faced her again, lifted an eyebrow in an expression that said, *What now?*

She shouldn't have stopped him. Why had she done that? "Never mind. Go to bed."

"Not yet. You've got something on your mind. What?"

"It's stupid…"

"What?"

"Well, um, remember Lucy Doherty?"

He was frowning, puzzled. And why shouldn't he be? Lucy Doherty was a page from the distant past. She had gone away to college over a decade ago, married some med student and moved to Colorado, if Joleen remembered right.

"What about her?" he asked.

"Was that…were you in love with her?"

He folded his arms over his broad chest. "Weird question."

She shrugged, to show him that she agreed with him. It *was* a weird question, and she shouldn't have asked it. She wished she hadn't.

But she had, so she might as well get his answer.

Not that he would give it easily. He said, "I was sixteen years old."

"Meaning...?"

"I don't get it. What made you think of Lucy?"

"Oh, I don't know..." *Liar,* a critical voice inside her head accused. *You are a stone liar.* "I was just wondering..." Wondering while you kissed me, remembering you and Lucy, the way I spied on *you* kissing *her*...

Yes. That was the truth of it. His kiss had reminded her of watching him with Lucy. But she simply could not make her mouth say that truth.

Why not? She could—and usually did—tell Dekker anything and everything. But somehow, she couldn't bring herself to tell him this particular truth, not right now, not tonight.

You do not *tell him everything,* that critical voice insisted. And the voice was right. Somehow she'd never gotten around to telling him how she'd spied on him with Lucy, though it had happened almost fifteen years ago, was a meaningless incident, really, nothing to make a big deal over.

Well, and now she considered the question, why *should* she have told him that? It *was* years and years ago. Before her father died, when she had felt...safe. Secure enough with her world and her place in it to do naughty things now and then. She had as good as forgotten all about it.

Until tonight. Until Dekker had kissed her. Not deeply. But long...

"Jo, are you all right?" He was watching her too closely, that frown of puzzlement still creasing his brow.

She drew herself up. "I am fine. And it is late. Go to bed."

He lingered for just a moment, on the verge of saying more. But then he only muttered a good-night and left her, shutting the door carefully behind him, so that all she heard was the tiny click as the latch caught.

Joleen turned off the lamp—Dekker had said they should keep the lights off—and she kicked off her shoes and stretched out on her bed to wait for him to have his turn in the bathroom.

A minute or two later she heard him in there, heard the water running, heard the toilet flush. He finished, as he'd promised, in almost no time at all.

There was silence from the other side of the door. The faint clicking sounds from the early-model digital clock on her nightstand seemed suddenly very loud.

She should get up, wash her face, brush her teeth. But she just lay there, staring into the darkness.

Joleen lifted a hand, touched the pads of her fingers first to the space between her brows and then, very lightly, to her lips. Her eyelids drifted down.

She turned on her side and snuggled into the pillow.

An interesting way to spend a wedding night, she thought as sleep came creeping up on her—alone in her own bed, touching the places her absent bridegroom had kissed....

Chapter Nine

By morning the reporters had discovered the address of the Bravo Baby's bride. A caravan of them followed the Lexus all the way to the airport.

Dekker didn't try to reason with them. He didn't yell at them to get lost. He didn't even rev up the Lexus and leave them eating his dust.

When Joleen praised his self-restraint, he replied with obvious satisfaction, "Where we're going, they won't be able to get to us."

Joleen began to understand what her husband meant, when they arrived at the airport and she learned that Jonas Bravo had sent a private plane for them. More than a plane. A jet.

"Jonas offered me the use of one of his planes when I flew home last week," Dekker said. "I turned him down, told him a commercial flight would do just fine.

And then I ended up spending the night at O'Hare, holding up DeDe's wedding in the process. Not this time. If I have to learn to live with reporters tailing me everywhere I go, damn it, I'll get there fast and in comfort."

They landed at Los Angeles International Airport at just a little past noon. A long, black limousine was waiting to take them to Jonas's house in Bel Air.

Angel's Crest looked like the villa of some Mediterranean king. Of pinkish stone, with a red tile roof, the house crowned a hill at the end of a long curving drive lined in stately palm trees. From the back, which was visible most of the way up the drive, it was all carved stone archways, jewel-paned glass and glittering fountains. Also in back, across a spacious courtyard from the house itself, a rectangular swimming pool tiled in cobalt blue sparkled like a huge sapphire, catching and throwing back the golden rays of the southern California sun.

The limousine topped the hill and drove around to the front, where the view was simpler than on the way up. The facade consisted of two wings of that pinkish stone, each with a double row of large windows, upstairs and down. The wings flanked an imposing portico a story taller than the rest of the house. The portico boasted a row of smooth stone pillars and a mosaic-tile floor.

Beyond the giant, studded mahogany front door, a beautiful black iron staircase curved upward toward an arched ceiling three stories above.

"Palmer," said Dekker to the man who answered the door. "How are you?"

"I am quite well, sir. Yourself?"

"Fine. This is my wife, Joleen."

"Hi." Joleen held out her hand.

Palmer hesitated only a fraction of a second before clasping Joleen's fingers and giving a quick squeeze. "A pleasure, Mrs. Bravo."

Sammy, who'd been clutching Dekker's index finger and staring wide-eyed until then, stepped forward. "I Sam."

The butler gazed down at him and spoke gravely. "How wonderful to make your acquaintance, young man." Palmer glanced up and met Joleen's eyes. "Miss Mandy will be so pleased to find she has a…" He paused, stuck on the exact nature of the relationship.

Joleen came to his aid. "Nephew. Mandy is Sam's aunt. Stepaunt, I guess, if you want to get specific about it."

"Yes, of course. Her nephew. That's right." Palmer gestured toward the curving staircase. "May I show you to your rooms?"

Dekker asked, "My brother…?"

"He should be here soon, with Mrs. Bravo—that is, the *other* Mrs. Bravo. They've requested a late lunch—at two, in the small dining room, if that will suit you?"

"Sounds great."

"You remember the way to the nursery?"

Dekker said he did.

"If the boy is agreeable, you could take him there before proceeding to the dining room. Amanda's nanny, Claudia, will watch them both while the adults enjoy a more leisurely meal than would be possible with the little ones in attendance.''

Since Sam was usually pretty good in new situations, Joleen gave a qualified yes. ''We'll try it. Kind of play it by ear. See how he takes it.''

''Whatever you decide. Just an option, you understand.'' Palmer led them up the stairs and down a couple of hallways, finally stopping to usher them into a spacious bed/sitting room. ''I hope this will do.''

The room took Joleen's breath away. Lush floral fabrics covered the sofas and the bed. Gold-threaded brocade curtains spilled to the floor around the ceiling-high arched windows. A heavily carved gilt-framed mirror hung over a fireplace with a mantel that looked as if it might have once graced the private rooms of some decadent French king. Glass doors opened onto a terrace, which overlooked the city far below.

Joleen found herself staring at the bed. It was huge, king-size at least, silk pillows piled high against the padded satin headboard. It was also the only bed in the room.

''The closets and bath are through there.'' Palmer gestured toward a door on a wall perpendicular to the one that led out to the hall. ''And a room for the boy…'' He strode over and opened a third door. ''I had a bed with rails brought in—or is Sam still in a crib?''

''He's been in a bed for a couple of months now.''

''Excellent. You'll find a large bin of toys suitable for a boy Sam's age in there, as well.''

Sam picked up the important word, *toys,* and made a beeline for the room that had been set up just for him. Joleen followed as far as the door. She saw white-trimmed forest-green walls, a dark green rug on the burnished wood floor. It was cozy and inviting. And Sam was already digging into the toy box.

Joleen turned back to the adults in the main room. "It's just great," she said to Palmer. "You have thought of everything." Well. Everything except the fact that she and Dekker slept in separate beds...

The butler nodded. "Also, there's a smaller bath, on the other side of the child's room."

"Thanks, Palmer," Dekker said.

"You are quite welcome, sir. Your bags will be brought up right away."

Palmer left them.

Joleen felt Dekker's eyes on her. "One bed," she said softly.

"Yeah." His smile was rueful. "I noticed that."

"I take it you didn't tell your brother about our...situation?"

"That's right. Though I trust him." That was a rare thing, coming from Dekker. He was so cautious. He hardly trusted anyone.

"You know him that well? In the few days you spent here?"

"Yeah. I think I do. It's crazy, I know. A lot of it's just...a sense I have of him. An instinct. But there are also his actions. Like the way he handled himself when he tracked me down back home. He told me the facts straight out, no hedging around. When I refused to believe him, he didn't argue, just gave me his card, with all his private numbers on it, so I could reach him any time I wanted to. When I showed up here a few days later, he was ready for me. He's a very busy man, but somehow he found time for me. A lot of time. That's how he's been with me. Never pushing me, but right there, prepared to face whatever needed facing, as soon as I was willing.'' He sent her a sideways look. ''And I want to talk to him, about the problem with Robert Atwood. If that's all right with you.''

''You think he could help us?''

''I think he has resources and...methods of action at his disposal that we wouldn't even dream about. I have no doubt he could crush Atwood like a bug, if it came to that.''

Joleen looked at her friend with alarm. ''*Crush* him?''

''I meant financially, that Jonas would know how to ruin him.''

She sent a furtive glance toward the other room and lowered her voice so her son wouldn't hear. ''I'm not having any part in crushing Sammy's grandfather, financially, or otherwise, no matter how rotten a human being he might be.''

''Settle down, Jo. I said Jonas *could* crush him, not that I'd ask him to. I was trying to make the point that Jonas might provide other...options. Other ways to approach the problem.''

''Oh.'' She dropped onto one of the beautiful sofas and stared up at him, contrite. ''Sorry. I'm edgy, I guess. The plotting and planning just never seem to end.''

''I only want us to be as prepared as we can be.''

''I know you do. And I'm grateful, I really am.'' He was a wonderful friend to her. The very best. She straightened her shoulders. ''All right, then. I agree. We'll talk to your brother.''

''Good—but I still think we should keep the exact

terms of our marriage to ourselves, the same as you did with Camilla.''

Joleen had given him a complete report of her conversation with her mother. ''I don't really think it's the same. You know how Mama is. Sometimes she talks too much. It's different if your brother can keep the truth to himself.''

Dekker shook his head. ''Why lay that on him? Why make him responsible for keeping our secrets? No. If we're going to do this, we have to do it right. Everyone has to believe we are married in *every* way.''

But we are *not* married in every way, she thought, irritation rising again. Really, all they did lately was scheme. And since last night—their wedding night— it seemed that they were constantly dealing with the issue of sex, with the fact that they weren't having any and no one was supposed to know that they weren't.

Which was what they'd agreed on.

She'd better remember that.

Chin up, she told herself. It's a reasonable plan and we're going to stick to it. Stop feeling all put-upon and focus on solving the problem at hand.

She spoke briskly. ''Okay. We have more of us than beds to sleep in. What do you think we should do about it?''

''I can take Sam's room. And he can sleep in here with you.''

That sounded like a sensible solution. ''Okay, that should—''

Someone tapped on the outer door. Dekker went and let in two maids who were carrying their luggage.

"Just put it all right there." He indicated a spot near the door to the closets and the bath.

Dekker waited until the two women had left them alone again befcre he turned to Joleen. "On second thought..."

"What?"

"This house is crawling with service staff. If we sleep in separate rooms, my brother might never know—but the maids will."

She didn't see how the maids would find out anything. And she also didn't see that it mattered—which must have shown on her face.

He made a low, impatient noise in his throat. "Jo. They make the beds. They change the towels, empty the wastebaskets. They see everything. No matter how careful we are, after a couple of days, they will get the picture that you and Sam are sleeping in here—and I'm in there."

"Oh, come on. Does it really matter what the maids know?"

"Use your head. Why would we let some stranger in on a secret we're not willing to share with my brother or your mother?"

Scheming, she thought again. Plotting and planning. And always having to make sure everyone thought they were lovers when they were not.

"What is the maid gonna care?"

"The maid might care a lot. If the right person got to her. If she was paid enough to share what she knows."

"This is too much. You are kiddin' me."

He just looked at her, wearing that stony expression he got when he was not going to budge about something. She threw up both hands. "Well, fine. So what do we do?"

"Sam will have to stay in the other room. And the two of us will sleep in here."

Her heart did a funny little stutter inside her chest. "Together?"

He gave her a lazy grin. "Is that a request?"

She saw that he was teasing her, and felt relief—didn't she? "Very funny."

He was all seriousness again. "You get the bed. I'll take one of the couches. I'll just use a pillow and a blanket, and I'll put them away every morning before we go down to breakfast. All my things, though, will be in this room, with yours. We'll share the main bathroom. That should be enough to make it appear that we're also sharing the bed." He paused, then prompted, "Well? What do you think?"

"I think that you have been in the detective business for way too long."

"Maybe I have. That doesn't change the situation we have to deal with here. What do you say?"

What *could* she say? He was probably right. He usually was, in matters of this kind. "Okay, okay. We'll share this room. But I'm smaller than you. I'd probably be more comfortable than you would on the couch."

"Offer again, and I won't say no."

"We'll switch off. That's fair."

"Can't argue with that."

"Mama." Sam came toddling through the door to the smaller room. "Potty?"

He was in training pants. And he was doing just

great, too. Day by day, the accidents were fewer and farther between.

"Right this way." She caught his little hand and led him back through his room to the bath on the other side.

They took Sam to meet Mandy and her nanny before they went down to join Jonas and his wife. Mandy was a beauty, with thick black curls and dark eyes.

She fluttered her impossibly long eyelashes at them, then picked up a stuffed dragon and bopped Sam on the head with it. Sam grabbed it away from her and bopped her right back.

They stared at each other for a long and dangerous moment. And then they both grinned.

Mandy turned for the stacks of blocks in the corner. Sam waddled right along behind her.

"He'll be fine, *señora,*" promised the pretty young nanny.

Joleen's gaze was still on her son. "Sammy, we'll be back soon."

Sam didn't even glance her way. He was already squatted on the floor, helping Mandy add to her stacks of blocks.

Dekker muttered, "That kid really misses you when you go."

"No separation anxiety," she told him loftily, turning to look him square in the eye. "That is a good thing. My son is secure with his world and his place in it."

Dekker kept a straight face, but those midnight eyes were gleaming. "I never doubted that."

"You'd better not." She reached out, took his arm.

It was such a simple gesture, something she'd done a hundred times before.

But this time it was…different. A tiny thrill passed through her, a shiver laced with fire. And she found she was all too aware of the feel of his forearm under her hand, the texture of the hair there, the warmth of his skin, the hard muscle beneath.

And Dekker had picked up her reaction—though it was achingly obvious he didn't understand it. He frowned down at her, baffled. "Jo?"

She laughed and tossed her head—to clear it of this sudden crazy notion that touching Dekker excited her.

"You okay?" He was eyeing her with extreme wariness.

She flashed him her brightest smile. "Better get downstairs, don't you think?"

"But are you sure you—"

"Dekker, let's go. Your brother is waiting."

Jonas Bravo looked a lot like Dekker. Uncannily so, Joleen thought when Dekker reintroduced them. He had those deep-blue eyes that looked black as midnight from certain angles. And that cleft in his square chin.

The two were built a lot alike, too—big—with thick, wide shoulders and muscular arms. So odd she hadn't noticed the resemblance that first time she'd met Jonas, a couple of weeks ago, when he and his wife had shown up at her mama's door.

But she'd been so distracted that day, with all the details that went into planning a wedding. And she hadn't been looking for Dekker's long-lost big brother to come knocking out of nowhere. She'd believed as she'd always believed: that Dekker was Lorraine Smith's beloved only son. And she had *seen* what she believed.

Amazing how much things could change in the space of two weeks.

Joleen had liked Jonas's wife right from the first. At second meeting, she saw no reason to alter her opinion of Emma Bravo, who had chin-length hair the color of moonbeams, a taste for bright colors and tight, short skirts—and a smile as big as Texas, which was her home state.

Dekker teased Emma that he'd missed her the last time he'd been in town.

The beauty mark by Emma's red mouth disappeared as she grinned. "Jonas and I had a few things to...work out." She put her hand lightly on her husband's arm. The two shared a look that made the air shimmer with heat.

Jonas said, "She's decided she'll never leave me again."

Emma's smile was slow and knowing. "He is stuck with me now."

Joleen thought she'd never seen a man so happy to be stuck. And she felt a little stab of something that just might have been envy.

She heard her mama's words in her head. *Passion and excitement. And magic. I want those things for you—and I want them for Dekker, too....*

It was about as clear as the view through the window that looked out on the pool that Jonas and Emma had all those things. And more.

Joleen slid a glance at Dekker, who was looking at the other couple right then. And she couldn't help thinking of that moment upstairs in the nursery, when she'd taken his arm and shivered at the feel of him under her hand.

Had that really happened?

Well, of course it had.

She knew it had.

But what did it *mean?*

Oh, well, what a silly question. She knew what it meant.

Something had changed. Something had...shifted. It had started last night, with the long, sweet kiss at her kitchen table, the kiss he had intended only for the benefit of the man watching them from outside, the kiss that, Joleen was reasonably sure, had meant very little to her lifelong friend.

Too bad she couldn't say the same thing for herself.

Since that kiss, she had started seeing her best-friend-turned-husband in a whole different light. They'd barely been married for twenty-four hours. And already she was changing her mind about a few things.

Changing her mind in a large and scary way—which was probably the reason she'd felt so edgy, back in their bed/sitting room, when they got into it, *again,* on the issue of sleeping arrangements.

She was starting to wonder why they didn't just forget all about this big secret they were keeping. If they went ahead and slept together, there wouldn't *be* any secret to worry about. They would be married, in *every* way. It wouldn't matter who spied on them, who made the bed, or who changed the towels in the bathroom. It wouldn't matter if reporters or private detectives crept around outside their windows trying to get a glimpse of what was going on in there. All anyone who watched them would find was a pair of newly-weds doing exactly what newlyweds do.

But there was a big problem with that idea: Dekker himself. She recalled the baffled look he had given her when she'd touched him and felt what she'd always sworn she didn't feel—not with Dekker, not with her dear, dear friend.

He just didn't get it, didn't see what was happening to her.

He didn't *want* to get it.

Not that she could blame him. It wasn't part of the deal, for her to go and get turned on by him. She'd told him it would take her *years* before she'd allow herself to get involved with a man romantically again.

And he'd made it so carefully, painfully clear that he wasn't interested in anything like that, either. That he didn't believe he would *ever* be interested.

Dead meat, he had called himself. Emotional dead meat when it came to man-woman love…

What did that *mean,* exactly? She should have probed further on the subject, that night a week ago, when they'd first cooked up this marriage scheme in her mother's dark backyard.

Was he…did he mean that he *couldn't?* That he wasn't capable, physically, of making love? Was it possible that the scars Stacey had cut into his heart went that deep? That he couldn't even share pleasure with a woman anymore?

Looking back on a few things Stacey had said during the really rough time at the end of their marriage, well, maybe there *had* been some problem in that area. Back then Joleen had chalked up those remarks to Stacey's natural tendency to overdramatize every little thing. And Stacey had been so…messed up, by then. So terribly confused and out of touch with reality. She had said a lot of things that bore no relationship at all to the truth.

So most likely Dekker had meant it more in the *emotional* sense. That, emotionally, he wanted nothing to do with man-woman love or anything that went with it. That *was* how he'd put it: *emotional* dead meat—or had he?

Had *he* been the one to use the word, *emotional?* On deeper reflection, she couldn't be sure. It might have been Joleen herself, putting her own spin on what he had told her.

Down the table Emma laughed. She was talking about the business she owned, a pet grooming shop in Beverly Hills. She and Jonas were making plans to open more of them.

And Dekker had turned. He was looking at her now. He had one brow lifted. Joleen knew he was wondering what she could possibly be thinking about. She sent him a quick, tight smile, shifted her glance away, picked up her fork and turned her attention to finishing her meal.

At least, she pretended to concentrate on the food.

But her mind really was a thousand miles away, tracking the past—the events that had shaped them. The people who had made them what they were.

Well, not *people*. One person.

Stacey…

Chapter Ten

Dekker rarely would talk about Stacey. But Joleen knew most of the story, anyway.

After all, Stacey had been Joleen's friend first. And when things got bad, Joleen was the one Stacey came to in her misery, the one Stacey confided in.

And Stacey had not always been so…difficult. So desperate and sad. At the beginning, well, she was really something. So much fun…

Like a sudden light in a dark room, blinding but welcome. That was Stacey. Joleen had been drawn to her from the moment they met—at Central States Academy of Cosmetology, when they were both nineteen.

There was something purely magical about Stacey. Something bigger than real life. It was as if she wove a spell, with the music of her laugh and the aura that surrounded her, an aura of excitement and…what? *Specialness,* maybe.

Stacey was everything Joleen wished she could let herself be. Stacey never had small emotions. She cried and laughed with total abandon. She never fretted. Never worried—or that was how she came across at first. She and Joleen were about the same size, both had brown hair and dark eyes. But the resemblance ended there.

Stacey was a little like Joleen's mother and sisters. Prone to making big drama out of the smallest events. Stacey loved roller coasters, for heaven's sake. And she had a *tattoo,* which had seemed to Joleen to be so wonderfully brazen and daring. At tattoo of a blood-red snowflake, low down on her back, so low down it was really more on her bottom—the left side, just above the dimple.

"Snowflakes are the most perfect, most beautiful thing in nature," Stacey told Joleen. "And no two of them are ever alike. And they don't last, they are gone in a moment, melting on your tongue. Except for *my* snowflake. I'll have it my whole life."

Which, as it turned out, hadn't been all that long.

The truth was, Dekker and Stacey were a disaster together. Their love was hot and passionate and all consuming. Their marriage had been a runaway train—something big and powerful and out of control, plummeting down from the crest of a high mountain, headed for a crash of stupendous proportions.

And Joleen was the one who had introduced them. On Easter Sunday. At her mama's house.

Stacey didn't have any family to speak of. Her parents had divorced when she was seven. Her mother had remarried and lived in Colorado somewhere. Stacey didn't know where her dad was. She hadn't seen him in ten years, she said. Stacey said she loved how, even though Joleen's dad had died, the family hadn't broken up. Joleen and her mother and her sisters still shared the family home. Joleen had aunts and uncles, from both sides, and they all got together on a regular basis. Stacey said she *longed* for that kind of family connection.

Stacey came for dinner that Easter, when she and Joleen were both nineteen. And Dekker came, too.

He'd been a little late, as Joleen remembered it. He'd had his own place for four or five years by then. But he was a dutiful son and would often visit his mother—or, rather, the woman they had all believed at the time was his mother.

And he would always try to make it over for family events. Then again, he *had* been ambitious back then. Totally dedicated to getting ahead. He'd worked long hours with the OCPD, and sometimes he just couldn't get away.

He had come to dinner that Easter, though. He had walked into the house and set his eyes on Stacey, and that was that.

"Who's your friend, Joly-Poly?"

Joly-Poly. He used to call Joleen that, back then. She hated it. Joly-Poly. Roly-poly. They sounded way too much the same. And roly-poly, everybody knew, meant fat—which Joleen was not. Or it meant those little gray armadillo-backed bugs that squeezed up into a tight little ball if you touched them.

She'd answered him grudgingly. "This is Stacey. And you'd better be nice to her."

"Oh, I will. Real nice. As nice as I can be."

Joleen had seen it all, then. In the way Dekker was looking at Stacey—and the way that Stacey was staring back at him, all that specialness, that magic she had, shining in her eyes. Zap. Hit by the thunderbolt, like in that old movie, *The Godfather,* both of them. Goners.

They were married six weeks later. And almost immediately things had started going wrong....

"Right, Jo?" she heard Dekker say.

Joleen blinked. "I...pardon me?" She gave her husband her brightest smile.

He looked at her as he had in the nursery—as if he was worried about her. And as if she made him a little bit nervous.

But that look only lasted a fraction of a second. She doubted their hosts had even noticed it.

"I said, the reporters don't bother you, the way they get to me."

She picked up her water goblet and sipped from it, giving herself a minute to pull her wandering mind fully back to the here and now. "That's right." She set the goblet down. "But then, I've only had them tailing me since yesterday. I'm sure it's not gonna take long until I'll be as fed up with them as Dekker is."

Emma sighed. "When Jonas and I got married, it was the same. I couldn't take a step without tripping over some news hound."

"It became necessary," Jonas said, "to throw the hounds a bone."

Dekker took his meaning. "A press conference."

"Right. We'll set one up for Monday or Tuesday.

You talk to them on your terms, in a formal setting. Tell them how happy you are, how much in love, whatever you're willing to let them know. The point is, you can plan ahead what you're going to say to them. *You* control the situation. Give them enough to make a decent story and they'll leave you alone—for a while, anyway.''

"At this point, I'll try anything," said Dekker.

"As I said, we'll set it up ASAP."

Dekker slanted Joleen a look. She read the question in his eyes. He was wondering if she was ready to talk about the Atwood situation.

Joleen nodded. "Might as well get it over with."

Emma laughed. "What is this? Get *what* over with?"

Dekker said, "We have…another issue we could use some advice on."

"Tell us."

So Dekker told them. He did the job much more simply and efficiently than Joleen could have managed—only leaving out the connection between their sudden marriage and Robert Atwood's ultimatum. And, of course, the depressing details of their sleeping arrangements.

Joleen felt the eyes of her host and hostess on her more than once during the telling. And she had a sense that they both easily deduced what Dekker was leaving out—well, maybe not the secret of their nonexistent sex lives, but certainly the fact that they had married to give Joleen a better defense against Robert Atwood's potential claims of her unfitness as a mother.

"It sounds to me as if you've made all the right moves," Jonas said when Dekker had finished. "Stay married—happily, of course. Provide the best of everything for that little boy. And by that I mean a good, stable, loving home as well as all the obvious things that your money will buy. If you do all that, I'd say that bastard can't touch you.''

''I thought so, too,'' Dekker agreed.

''I think we should go ahead and see Ambrose on Monday, though,'' Jonas said. ''I'm about 99 percent certain he'll tell us there's nothing else to do until Sam's grandfather makes his next move. But there's no harm in checking with him, in case there's something we're not seeing here.''

Emma must have noticed Joleen's questioning look. She explained, ''Ambrose McAllister handles all the personal legal matters for the Bravo family. He's been doin' it for more than thirty years. He is the sweetest, dearest man. And smart as they come, too. You will love him.''

Joleen tucked her napkin in at the side of her empty plate. ''I truly do appreciate all this.''

Emma grinned. ''No thanks are needed.'' She pushed back her chair and stood. ''Now, let's head on upstairs. I have a nephew up there and I want to meet him.''

It was the kind of day Joleen had read about and seen in movies: a real California day. Not a cloud in the sky and seventy-eight degrees at four in the afternoon.

Emma suggested it might be fun if they all went on out to the pool. She said they didn't need to go back to their rooms to change.

''You all can just choose what you need from the

cabanas. Palmer always keeps them stocked like a department store, with everything from bathin' suits in all sizes to air mattresses, goggles and snorkeling gear.''

Joleen laughed. ''What about sunscreen?''

''Honey, that's in there, too. Name your brand.''

So they all trooped out to the pool area, which had three cabanas, one for men, one for women—and one that was done up just like the poolside bar at some fancy hotel. Emma even went and got her dogs—a couple of cute and very well-mannered miniature Yorkshire terriers that she explained had first belonged to Jonas and Dekker's mother, Blythe.

The dogs sat in the shade of the loggia, which was a long colonnaded back porch beneath the big terrace off the master bedroom suite. The dogs looked so sweet and eager, wagging their tails and panting with happiness, as if just being there tickled them pink.

The humans, on the other hand, suited up and swam in the cobalt-blue pool. Mandy and Sam splashed around on inflatable toys in the shallows, with the nanny there to tend to their every whim.

With Sam so well taken care of, Joleen even dared to stretch out on an air mattress and close her eyes for a few minutes. It was a little bit of heaven, just floating there in the blue, blue pool under the paler blue of the California sky.

But then she felt the slight tug on the side of the mattress and knew without opening her eyes who it was.

She didn't move, didn't speak. Kept her eyes shut. Maybe, if she didn't acknowledge him, he would just swim away. For several long and lovely minutes, she had not even thought of him. It had been real nice, for a change, not to have her lifelong-friend-turned-husband-turned-object-of-impossible-desire dominating her every thought.

But then he had to go and dribble cool water over her sun-warmed thighs.

"Dekker," she muttered, "I am tryin' to relax here."

More water dribbled over her. She opened her eyes—just to slits, enough that she could see he was scooping water into his palm and pouring it on her in a trickling stream.

"Stop," she said.

He didn't.

She turned her head and met those eyes that, right then, seemed to just about exactly match the cobalt blue of the pool. He was grinning, like a naughty kid up to mischief and enjoying it.

"What part of 'stop' was unclear to you?"

The grin faded. "Something's bugging you." He spoke low, for her ears alone. "What?"

"Nothing is—" She cut herself off. Lately, she'd been telling way too many lies. But not to Dekker. She never lied to Dekker. Was she going to start now?

He was waiting, treading water inches from her air mattress, dark hair slick and shiny as the pelt of a seal, water drops gleaming in his brows and lashes, dripping in little rivulets down the strong column of his neck.

A forbidden urge assailed her—to lean close, stick out her tongue, lick the water right off his neck, then slide her tongue upward, over that wonderful dent in his chin and straight to his lips.

"Damn it, Jo. What is going on?"

She snapped her guilty gaze away from his mouth—
and up to meet his accusing eyes. "I..." She sent a
swift glance around them. Jonas and Emma were sitting side by side, on the edge at the deep end, dangling
their legs in the water, with eyes only for each other.
The kids and the nanny paddled happily in the shallows.

No one was looking at them. But still, it was hardly
the time or the place to talk about this—if there even
was such a time, such a place...

Trailing gleaming drops of water, Dekker lifted a
hand and clasped her arm just below the elbow. It was
a touch intended to reassure, she knew. A touch that
meant, *I'm here. You can trust me. You can talk to
me.*

But it didn't work.

Because heat went zinging through her, a bullet of
longing, ricocheting up to her shoulder, zipping back
and forth around her heart and then zooming on down
to her belly—and lower.

"Don't!" She jerked away.

Dekker stared at her for a long, awful moment. It
was a stunned, angry stare—and an injured one, too,
as if she had done more than jerk away from him. As
if she had slapped him right across the face.

Then he turned around in the cool, clear water and
swam away from her.

Chapter Eleven

Something had happened, with Jo. Something was wrong. Dekker didn't know what.

She wouldn't tell him. Once she gave him the brush-off, there in the pool, she started avoiding him. Avoiding his eyes, avoiding physical contact.

Around six, when the nanny took the kids in to feed them, Jo excused herself, too. She vanished into the house for the good part of an hour. The rest of them were just coming inside when she appeared again, freshly showered, smelling like flowers, wearing a clingy scoop-necked dress the same golden-brown color as the lights in her hair when the sun got caught in it. The dress skimmed all her curves and fell to just above her ankles.

Emma said what Dekker was thinking. "Girl, you are lookin' good."

Joleen smiled her thanks at the compliment, and then Emma explained that she and Jonas were going to have to leave their guests to their own devices for a while. "We have *got* to freshen up." Emma slid her husband a sly look. The glance he gave her in return made it pretty clear that more than freshening up would be going on as soon as he got his wife alone. "Dinner in the small dinin' room at eight-thirty. We'll have drinks in the living room off the grand foyer, at eight—that is, if that's all right with the two of you?"

"Sounds great," Jo answered.

"Yeah, great," Dekker muttered, instantly wishing he could call the words back, try them again, make them sound a little more upbeat.

But he wasn't feeling all that upbeat at the moment. Damn it, he wanted to know what was eating Jo.

And Emma and Jonas didn't care about his bad attitude, anyway. Right then, as far as those two were concerned, the rest of the world flat-out did not exist. Emma curled her hand around her husband's arm and led him away.

Which left him and Jo, standing there alone just beyond the set of French doors that led out to the loggia. It was a chance, he realized, to find out what her problem was.

But before he could say a word, she started giving him orders. "Go on up and have your shower," she instructed, as if he were some kid who had to be reminded when he needed a bath. "I'll see how Sam's doin'." She turned and walked away from him.

He should have stopped her, should have said, *Hey, wait a minute. What the hell is going on here?* But he didn't. He just stood there, wishing he could strangle someone, watching her walk away. That damn dress clung to her backside like poured honey. And it had a slit, too. Right up the back, all the way to her knees. He could see the smooth, ripe skin of her calves as she moved. He must have stood there for a good sixty seconds, till she was way out of sight, staring like a long-gone fool at the place where she had last been.

He just wasn't used to this—to Jo shutting him out. Not in the past few years, anyway. Yeah, when she was a kid she used to put on attitudes with him. She would get all insulted at something he'd said. Wouldn't tell him what he'd done to make her mad, or anything sensible like that. She'd just get steamed up and not speak to him for days or even weeks.

Which hadn't bothered him a whole hell of a lot back then. She was a kid and she had more to deal with than any kid should, after her dad died. He figured she had a lot of frustrations bottled up, from always having to be the responsible one in her family. And he figured he could take it if she wanted to exercise her frustrations on him.

But the days of her putting on attitudes with him were behind them. Had been for a long time. Or so he'd thought until this afternoon—when she'd given him attitude to spare.

Why? He needed to get to the bottom of it.

That night, he decided. When they were alone, after the drinks and the dinner and all that, when they finally went up to bed. She'd have a hard time evading him then, since they would be sleeping in the same damn room.

The hours seemed to crawl by until that time came, even though Jonas and Emma were terrific hosts and the food was exceptional. After the meal they went to the media room, where they watched a bizarre but entertaining film about aliens—both the illegal variety and the kind from outer space. Emma explained that Jonas had been the movie's major backer. The filmmaker was evidently Jonas's close personal friend.

Joleen sat at Dekker's side through both the meal and the movie. She laughed in all the right places. She chatted easily with his brother and Emma. She even talked to *him*, now and then, soft little murmurings. Things like "Please pass the bread" and "Thank you" and "Excuse me," when her napkin slid off her lap and she bent over to get it and her leg brushed his under the table.

She never would look at him, though. Not *really* look at him. Her eyes were always sliding away whenever he tried to snare her glance.

So all right. Later. He'd deal with her later. When they were finally alone.

At a little after midnight they said good-night to Jonas and Emma. They stopped in at the nursery to get Sam, who'd already had his bath and been dressed in his pj's. The little guy had fallen asleep in a nest of pillows on the floor of the playroom. Dekker carried him back to their own rooms, where Jo tucked him into bed. She tiptoed from the smaller room and quietly shut the door.

It was time, and he knew it. Time to confront her. Time to get whatever it was out in the open where they could deal with it.

But there was a slight problem.

He did not have a clue where to begin.

She said, "You go ahead. Use the bathroom first."

"No. It's all right. I can wait."

"No really, you go on."

They stood there, in the area between the foot of the bed and the grouping of big, soft, gorgeous sofas, staring at each other.

Finally she let out a sound—a small noise in her throat that spoke of pure impatience with him, with the situation, with who the hell knew what all. "Oh, all right, Dekker. I'll go first."

"Good," he said, his tone as gruff and fed up as he felt right then. "Do it."

She turned for the big closet and dressing area that led to the bathroom, and when she got in there, she shut the door behind her. Which left him alone in the bed/sitting room, staring at the shut door and facing the bleak truth.

He just…didn't know how to get through to her.

She was the talker, damn it. She was the open one, the easy one, the one who never hesitated when it came time to hash something out.

He never had to do more than lift an eyebrow or mutter, What? And she would be telling him any and everything she had on her mind.

So what the hell had happened? What had gone wrong? Had he *done* something to get her mad?

He couldn't think what.

However, somehow, since late this afternoon, muttering What? and raising his eyebrows had gotten him exactly nowhere with her. He'd even gone so far, down there in the pool, as to ask her directly what was going on. For that, he got half a denial.

At least she'd done that much. Stopped herself in

midlie. He could do without hearing lies from her mouth.

Dekker stalked over to one of those big, beautiful couches and dropped into it, swinging his feet up and plunking them down on the gleaming wood of the inlaid coffee table. He looked at his shoes, though he wasn't really seeing them.

He was thinking that Jo had damn well better *not* start telling him lies. He'd had enough lies in his life. Enough lies and enough sulking. Enough of the kind of woman who needed more of everything than he could ever give. The kind of woman who made him feel that he was lacking, somehow, that he couldn't quite cut it—as a husband, as a man, as a caring human being.

The kind of woman that Stacey had been.

Hell, was he cursed or something? He couldn't help but start to wonder. Right now, it seemed as if all he had to do was marry a woman to turn her into a—

Dekker shut his eyes.

No. Not right. Not fair.

Jo was not Stacey. Not in a hundred thousand years.

And Stacey, well, in the end, no matter how mixed-up she'd been, and no matter how exhausting the emotional chase she had led him, he *had* chosen her, loved her, pursued her. Married her.

And he'd been no more ready to be a husband than she had been to be a wife. They'd made a royal mess of it. She had wanted his undivided attention, twenty-four hours a day. She'd wanted him to live, sleep, eat and *breathe* Stacey. And for a while he had given her just what she wanted.

But he was a man with a plan then. He had things

he wanted, too. Like to make detective, which meant time away from Stacey. Which made Stacey very unhappy.

He learned, as time went by, that Stacey not only *wanted* his attention. She needed it. Craved it. The way a drunk needs his bottle, the way a junkie requires a regular fix.

And damn it, he was not a bottle of scotch. He was not a hit of smack. He just couldn't do it, feed that hunger of hers indefinitely.

He knew now he should have tried to get her some help. But at the time, it was hard to see anything very clearly. At the time, his reaction had been to pull away.

And the more he pulled away, the more she *needed*. The more she cried and ranted and raved, accusing him of not loving her, not wanting her, not *being there* for her.

She staged some crazy stunts in her ongoing quest to get his undivided attention.

She'd tried getting him good and jealous.

If they went out to dinner, she'd flirt with the guy at the next table, so charmingly—and so blatantly—that the guy would get up and follow her when she went to the women's room. They would end up in the parking lot, Dekker and his wife's new admirer, duking it out—or at least, that's how it went the first four or five times she pulled that one.

But eventually Dekker got wise. As soon as she had picked out a sucker at another table, he would get up and leave her there.

So she changed tactics. She became totally devoted to him. She drowned him in her damned devotion, hanging on his every word, cooking lavish meals. She developed a kind of radar about those big meals of hers. Whenever he was working an important, time-consuming case, she would cook a lot of them. He would work late and miss them. And she would be crushed.

The total devotion lasted for a long time. And then, after one of their big fights when he didn't show up to eat another of her gourmet feasts, she disappeared. He came home the next night and she was gone. She left a note on fine linen stationery scented with her perfume. It said she "couldn't take it anymore." She "wasn't sure if she could even go on."

That note scared the hell out of him. She'd done some crazy things, but she'd never hinted at suicide before.

He was frantic, certain she meant to do something to hurt herself and desperate to make sure that she was all right. It was two in the morning.

He'd gone straight to Jo, pounded on the door of her mama's house, where she was still living then, not giving a damn if he woke up Camilla and the other girls.

But the others didn't wake. Or if they did, they stayed in their beds. Jo was the one who came to the door in her pajamas and robe, rubbing the sleep from her eyes.

He'd demanded to know where his wife was.

Jo pulled him inside, led him to the kitchen, made coffee and set a steaming mug of it in front of him.

Then she said she didn't know where Stacey had gone.

"She was here, then? You talked to her?"

"Drink your coffee, Dekker. Settle down."

"Did you *ask* her, try to find out where the hell she planned to go next?"

Jo dropped into the chair across from him. She stared at him for a moment that seemed to stretch out for at least a year. At last she nodded. "Yes. Yes, I did ask her."

He fisted his hands to keep from lurching across the table, grabbing her out of that chair and shaking her until everything she knew came spilling out. "And?"

"Oh, Dekker, what she said to me was between us. I just don't know if I should be talkin' to you about it. I don't know if it's the right thing to—"

"Tell me, damn you. I have to know."

Jo folded her hands on the table and looked down at them. Now she was shaking her head. "Stacey said…she said she couldn't trust me. She said that I would only end up telling you." Jo looked up then, a sad little smile curving her mouth. "It's strange, you know? But you and me, we go back such a long ways. You are *family* to me, Dekker. And Stacey, well, she is a dear, dear friend. I love her and I *hurt* for her, for everything she's goin' through. But it is not the same. And she *knew* that. Better than I did, I guess, until she said it to me…." Her voice trailed off. She was looking at her hands again.

Impatience tightened inside him like a fist. "Said *what* to you?"

Her head snapped up. Shadows haunted her eyes and her mouth trembled. "Oh, I don't—" She cut off the protests herself that time. And she told him, "Stacey said that my basic loyalty was to you. That when you came here lookin' for her, you would get me to tell you whatever I knew, no matter if I swore to her that I would never betray her trust.''

''It's not betraying her trust if you talk to me. You know it's not. She's not thinking clearly. And I have to find her. You have to tell me whatever you know.''

''I don't really know anything, honestly. She was here. She was upset. She would not say where she planned to go next.''

''Why the hell didn't you call me the minute she walked out your front door?''

''She asked me not to.''

''And you did what she asked?'' He sneered those words, glaring at her. ''Damn it, what are you, a stone idiot?''

She didn't rise to the bait. Even worried sick over his missing wife, he noticed that. She only met his gaze across her mama's breakfast table, her own eyes steady, her expression soft and sad with understanding.

Yeah. What really stuck with him, looking back now on that grim night, was how hard Jo had tried to make it easy on him. She hadn't fought back when he had insulted her. She hadn't ranted at him, though she could have made a case in her own mind that he deserved to hear a little ranting. She hadn't laid it on him hard, saying it was for his own good. She hadn't copped a single huffy, holier-than-thou attitude.

Because by that night, Jo had grown-up. The touchy, insecure teenager was gone. Somehow, while he hadn't been looking, while he'd been busy reeling through his life, trying to get ahead on the OCPD and be Stacey's husband at the same time, Jo had become a woman—and the kind of woman who refused to judge others, who could take a few verbal blows from a friend in need without feeling she had to retaliate.

She'd put it to him so gently, chosen her words with great care. Stacey had cried on her shoulder, she'd said. Stacey had talked about how things weren't working out.

But Jo's sweet kindness to him that night hadn't kept him from knowing what had really gone on. He knew his wife too well, knew that Stacey would have wailed and moaned. She would have called him a hardhearted SOB who refused to love a woman the way she needed to be loved.

"She'll be all right, Dekker," Jo had promised him. "She'll come back. I know she will...."

And she had come back. Six days later. Looking like hell, like she'd been at some weeklong party somewhere doing things he was probably better off never knowing about.

But alive. In one piece.

There had been a big scene, another in the infinite chain of big scenes. At the end she had begged him to take her back. She'd sworn she would never pull anything like that again.

And she hadn't.

Next, she started calling him at the station, leaving messages with the dispatcher.

"Please. You have to help me. Tell him he has to come home immediately. It's an emergency. It's life and death...."

The dispatcher would radio him and he would go charging back to the house—to find her sitting on the couch in a sexy nightgown, ready to show him her snowflake tattoo.

By then he had zero interest in her tattoo. Or in any part of her pretty, scented, smooth little body. He didn't want to make love with her. He didn't know if he would ever want to make love with her again—or with any woman, for that matter. The equipment, it seemed, had stopped working.

And he really didn't give a damn. A sort of numbness had set in. Which was okay with him. Numbness was a big improvement over the grueling agony of loving Stacey. It was a relief, more than anything. He was through, done, finished. No longer able to rise to the occasion.

His body was telling him something. It was time to surrender the field, to give up on the impossible task of trying to love a woman who could never get enough.

He found himself an apartment and moved out.

There were more big, teary scenes. For Stacey, anyway. He opted out of them. He would hang up the minute he heard her voice on the phone, hear her moaning and sobbing and begging him to give her just one more chance. He would refuse to open the door when she came pounding on it, calling his name, demanding that he open up and talk to her.

She had needed help. She had needed help every bit as much as a drowning woman needs someone to throw her a lifeline. But he'd been no help at all to her. He'd been too desperate himself—to keep from going down with her.

Jo had done better with Stacey—been more of a friend than he had ever been a husband. She'd thrown the damn lifelines. She'd taken Stacey to a counselor and arranged for her to join some kind of group therapy sessions. But Stacey had screwed it up. She would miss her appointments with the counselor. She wouldn't show up at group. The counselor had finally dropped her. The group had voted her out.

And she'd kept calling him, begging him, pleading with him to come back to her.

Her final call to him wasn't that much different from some of the calls that went before it. By then, it wasn't anything new when she said that she couldn't take it anymore. That if he didn't talk to her, she was going to end it.

He wasn't there to take that call. She left her last message for him on his answering machine. In it, she accused him of all the same old things—of deserting her, of not loving her, of not being there when she needed him most. She cried that she had had enough, more than she could take, of life and everything that went into it. She said she would wait ten minutes and if he didn't get back to her, she was swallowing a bottle of pills and she was going to bed. For good.

By the time he got that message, seven hours later, she was deep in the coma from which she would never wake.

The door across the room opened.

Jo came padding through it, barefoot, wearing a white cotton robe that reached her knees. Her face was scrubbed clean of makeup, and her hair curled, soft and full, around her heart-shaped face.

"Your turn," she said, her tone too bright—forced. Not right.

"Jo."

The tight little smile she was giving him vanished.

She hovered there, several yards away from him, near the end of the huge bed. Those big brown eyes were bigger than ever right then, dark and soft and full of all the things that, for some reason, she wouldn't tell him.

It came to him, hit him all over again, as if for the first time, in a flash of painful insight that constricted his throat and made his chest feel too small for the heart trapped inside it.

She was *his* lifeline. As much as she'd ever tried to be Stacey's. She had saved him from going down after Stacey died. She had come to him with her casseroles and her perky talk, with her insistence that he get out of the apartment, go to a movie, to a car show, to art festivals on the lawns at OCC, to flea markets at the state fairgrounds. She must have hauled out the damn *Sunday Oklahoman* every week for three or four months, there, and scanned all the ads and articles, picking out places she could drag him to. And then, after she picked them out, she worked on him, gently and without mercy, never giving up until he would finally agree to go there with her.

That was a friend.

They didn't come any better.

And he couldn't bear...this distance. This *strangeness,* between them.

He swung his feet off the coffee table and stood. He still didn't know how to make her talk to him, how to get rid of whatever it was that had come between them.

But the distance. He could do something about that. He could close it.

He went to her. She watched him coming, eyes that couldn't get any wider, somehow doing just that.

When he stood about two feet from her, where he could see the gold flecks in those wide, wide eyes, smell soap and a faint, sweet perfume—and peppermint toothpaste, when she let out a long, jittery breath—he made himself ask her. Again.

"What the hell is it? What's bothering you?"

She lifted a hand and put it against her throat. He saw the war going on inside her. She was thinking up lies, deciding whether or not to try running them past him.

He shook his head at her, slowly, tenderly. "Don't do it. Don't lie to me..."

She took that hand from her throat, waved it, as if she didn't know what to do with it.

He caught it. She stiffened. He thought, for a split second, that she would do what she had done to him down in the pool: jerk away, whisper hotly "Don't!"

But no. She caught herself. Her lashes swooped down. She dragged in another long, shaky breath and let it out with great care. Deliberately she twined her fingers with his.

Better, he thought. Now we're getting somewhere....

Her lashes fluttered up. She looked at him anxiously. "Let's...um. Could we sit down, do you think?"

He almost smiled. "Yeah. I think we could." The bed had no footboard, just the big padded satin affair at the head. "How about right here?" He sat on the end of it and pulled her down beside him. She came somewhat reluctantly, as if she'd thought better of the idea, but didn't know how to get out of it now.

It didn't matter if she hesitated, he told himself. She *did* sit. Beside him. She had laced her fingers with his. And now she would tell him what the hell was happening with her.

She spoke. "Um. Dekker…"

He gave her hand a reassuring squeeze. "Those are very nice feet you have. But do you think you could make yourself look at me?"

She did it, with obvious effort. "I…" She let out a small, anguished-sounding moan. "Oh, I just can't. I really can't, Dekker. Please try to understand…."

"Can't what?"

"Can't…talk about this, not right now. Please. Just don't make me. If you would only…"

"What? If I would only what?"

"Just…believe me when I tell you, it is not your fault. It is nothin' you have done. It is *my* problem. And I am going to handle it the best way I know how."

"Which is?"

She pulled her hand from his, waved it in the air some more. "No. I mean it. You have got to give me a little time here, okay?"

"Time for…?"

"To deal with it. To…work it out in my mind."

He almost demanded, *Work* what *out?* But he shut his mouth over those words. She was asking for time.

As her friend—hell, as her *husband*—it was his duty to see that she got what she needed. He owed it to her, for the sake of all that they were to each other, to wait until she felt that she could tell him this deep, dark secret of hers.

After a minute of strained silence, he muttered, "All right," then added more forcefully, "When?"

"When what?"

"When can you talk to me?"

She looked absolutely miserable. He wanted to grab her and...what? Pull her close. Protect her forever. Promise her that everything would be okay.

And then force her, somehow, to tell him. All of it. Whatever it was that she thought was so awful she couldn't even share it with him.

Nothing could be that awful. She ought to know that. There was nothing she could tell him that he couldn't take.

And besides, if she *did* tell him, well, maybe he could fix the problem, could *make* it okay....

But no.

He was not going to grab her. He was going to remember, to keep foremost in his mind all that she had done for him. Always, if he possibly could, he would honor her wishes.

He waited.

Finally she told him in a small, unhappy voice. "Soon. I promise. I will work this out and then we will talk about it."

"Soon," he echoed, wondering with a stab of impatience what exactly she meant by that.

"Yes." She was looking at her feet again, her voice small, sad and lost. "Soon..."

Chapter Twelve

Dekker took his turn in the bathroom and then they went to bed—Joleen *in* the bed, Dekker on one of the couches across the room. Joleen had a hard time getting to sleep. She wondered if Dekker was awake, too. Not a sound came from his side of the room. Could be he was just a very silent sleeper.

Or maybe he was lying over there on the cramped sofa in the dark, wondering what her problem was and when she would finally break down and tell him.

Oh, she didn't think she ever could.

How would she do it? How would she…get her mouth around the words?

Well, Dekker, the problem is, I have got the hots for you….

Not.

Or *I have rethought this whole separate beds thing,*

*and I have changed my mind about it. I would rather
you just come on over here and climb into bed with
me so that I can jump your bones....*

*I mean, that is, if you would like your bones jumped
by me. Would you? Could you...?*

Right.

No. Better to wait. At least for a while.

Maybe a way to tell him would come to her. Or
maybe these crazy new feelings she had for him would
just...go away. Maybe she'd get used to them. Learn
to live with them, to *cope* with them....

Oh, who did she think she was kidding?

Even if she woke up tomorrow and discovered that
these irksome new longings had vanished with the
light of day, Dekker was still going to want to know
what it had all been about.

But that would be all right, wouldn't it?

If only she didn't *feel* this way, if these little shivers
and flashes of heat would just stop quivering through
her when he touched her, when he *looked* at her, when
she looked at *him,* then they could laugh about it.

They could agree that it had only been a kind of
temporary insanity. They could talk it over and come
to some nice, neat, safe conclusion. They would decide that it was probably brought on by all the stress
in the past few weeks. Good old Jo had just snapped
for a little while there, gone delusional, imagined that
she wanted more from Dekker than he would ever be
willing to give.

She turned over, adjusted the covers, smoothed out
her pillow, tried not to sigh. She had a *little* time,
anyway. Before he would start pushing her again to
tell him what was going on in her head.

Maybe, in that time, some workable solution to this predicament would occur to her.

She sent a silent prayer to heaven that that might be the case. And after the prayer she lay very still, hoping sleep would find her.

It did, but not until a number of endless hours later.

Joleen woke with a start. It was morning. She had that where-am-I feeling. This was not her house, not her bed....

She was lying on her stomach. She lifted her head from the pillow and squinted at the satin headboard. "Ugh."

Before she could think better of the move, she rolled over and sat up.

That was when she saw Dekker. He was up—barely—standing over in the sitting area, wearing nothing but a pair of boxer shorts, folding up the blanket he had slept under. His hair was squashed on the left side, and he had a sleep dent on his cheek.

He looked...really good, in just his boxer shorts, as good as he'd looked yesterday, at poolside, in those swim trunks he'd borrowed from the men's cabana. He had powerful legs, that narrow waist, those heavy, wide shoulders corded with muscle.

And there it was—that shivery, infuriating thrill, zipping through her again.

So much for the false hope that it would all be over in the morning.

"'Mornin'."

He returned the greeting, then gestured toward the bathroom. "You want to...?"

"Are you, uh, plannin' to take a shower?"

"The thought had crossed my mind."

"Well, maybe, if I could just—"

"Go ahead."

"I will only be a minute."

"No big rush."

But she did rush. She rushed in there and she used the toilet and she washed her hands and she rushed back out. "Thanks. Your turn."

He laid the folded blanket over his arm, picked up his pillow and headed for the dressing area. When he got in there and shut the door, she sank to the edge of the bed with a tiny moan.

Oh, she hated this, all these stilted exchanges over the big, important issue of who would use the bathroom when. It was all so…dumb.

There was plenty of room in there, after all. That bathroom was like everything else at Angel's Crest. Fit for a king—and for his queen, too. That bathroom had two sinks, two showers, a huge tub with massaging jets and two commodes, each in its own little marble-walled cubicle. If they were *really* married, if they were doing *all* the things that married people do, they could go in there at the same time. They could each do whatever they needed to do without one of them in the least inconveniencing the other.

Or, if they only didn't have to *pretend* that they were *really* married, then she could share Sammy's bathroom, and Dekker could have the king-size one all to himself.

But no. They weren't *really* married and the maids could not be allowed to discover such a shocking fact.

She let out a huffy little breath—and decided she was making way too much out of this.

"Lighten up, girl," she said to the empty room. "It will all work out. Just give it time."

They shared the morning meal in the breakfast room, all four adults and the children, as well. Jonas suggested they fly to Las Vegas. "Just a day trip, the four of us. What do you think?"

"Jonas finds gambling relaxing," Emma said.

"That's right, I do. But if you two would rather do something else, just speak up."

Dekker said the idea was fine with him, and Joleen agreed that she would love to go. It sounded wonderful, she said.

Wonderful in more ways than one, she was thinking. They'd be good and busy, exploring the casinos, making their way among the crowds. There would be zero opportunity for private conversation. No time for her and Dekker to be alone, no time to dwell on the painful new awkwardness between them.

Leaving Sam and Mandy in the capable hands of the nanny, they headed for the airport at a little before eleven. The flight, in one of Jonas's aircraft, took hardly any time at all. They spent the better part of the afternoon wandering from one huge pleasure palace to the next. Jonas and Dekker played craps. Emma and Joleen yanked the one-armed bandit and tried a few hands of blackjack.

Some time after four they were recognized by an intense-looking fellow in plaid shorts with a fancy camera hung around his neck. Within ten minutes they had two other men a lot like the first one following after them.

"Time to go home," Jonas said wearily.

By seven they were back at Angel's Crest. They visited the nursery, then the four of them shared a late, light supper out on the loggia with the lights of L.A. and the blue of the Pacific spread out in a glittering panorama below.

The two couples retired to their rooms at nine-thirty. Dekker and Joleen stopping by the nursery to collect a sleeping Sam.

Once Sam had been tucked into his bed, there was the grueling who'll-use-the-bathroom-first routine to get through.

"Just go ahead."

"No, really, it's—"

"I mean it. Go on."

So Joleen went first. She took care to get the blanket and the pillow from the closet area on her way back out to the main room, since it was her turn to take the couch.

Dekker went into the dressing room as soon as she emerged from it. The minute the door closed behind him, she flew around the main room, turning off all the lights save one lamp beside the bed.

Then she plunked her pillow on the end of a sofa and lay down. Holding one side of the blanket and kicking the rest of it into place with a bicycling motion of her feet, she settled the blanket over her. She turned over on her right side, with her back to the room.

And she heaved a heavy sigh. Dekker was fast, when he used the bathroom getting ready for bed. She had wanted to be on the couch, under the blanket, in a position that would clearly signal she was on her way to sleep, before he returned. And she had succeeded.

Dekker emerged from the bathroom about three minutes later. She heard the whisper of his feet across the rug—and then nothing. He had stopped, was just standing there, midway between the dressing room door and where she lay on the sofa.

Joleen lay very still under her blanket, her eyes shut, willing him to say nothing, to go over to the bed and get into it and just...let it be.

She didn't quite get her wish. He swore. And he said her name.

She did not breathe. She did not move.

She was handling this all wrong and she knew it. She was hurting her dearest, truest, lifelong friend, leaving him to worry and wonder what could possibly be the matter with her.

But she couldn't bring herself to tell him.

And at the same time, she just didn't know how to pretend with him. How to act as if everything was normal, when it *wasn't* normal, when she was a wreck of unsatisfied yearning inside herself.

Just *wanting* a man shouldn't mess everything up like this. But somehow, it did. She couldn't relax with him, couldn't really *talk* to him. Not now. She knew that if she even tried, it would all come pouring out. She would embarrass herself and put poor Dekker on the spot.

She also knew the time was fast approaching when she would have to do just that.

But now all she wanted was to put it off. Avoid the inevitable. For a few days, a few hours, however long she possibly could.

She heard movement. He was walking away from her. He had given up, for now, on trying to talk to her.

There was a soft rustling—the blankets on the bed. And then a click as the room went dark.

On Monday, Jonas and Emma both had to work. Joleen spent a lot of that morning and afternoon in the nursery with the children, then later she gave the nanny a break and took them out to the pool. She didn't see much of Dekker, didn't know how he occupied himself.

Apparently, he had decided to give her what she'd said she needed—time and space to deal with what was bothering her.

At four, though, they were both due at the offices of Jonas's lawyer. They rode there together, in one of the long, black Bravo limousines. It was a silent ride. They looked out the smoky glass of the car's windows and avoided each other's eyes.

When they got to the offices of McAllister, Quinn and Associates, Attorneys at Law, a pretty, beautifully dressed secretary showed them to a conference room. Jonas and Ambrose McAllister joined them a few minutes later. The attorney, who was tall, white-haired and soft-spoken, listened to the same story Dekker had told Jonas and Emma two nights before.

When Ambrose had heard it all, he told them what Jonas had thought he might. He said they had done all that could be done until Robert Atwood made his next move.

"I want you to contact me immediately when that happens," Ambrose McAllister said. "We'll see what, exactly, we're going to be dealing with, and I'll advise you from there. Now. Is there anything else I can help you with? Anything at all?''

Dekker said he'd been thinking about changing his name, legally, to Bravo. ''After all, it's my real name, anyway.''

Ambrose nodded. ''And did you want to go back to Russell, as well?''

''No. I've been called Dekker so long, I don't think I want to try getting used to another first name.''

Joleen felt relief when he said that he'd keep his first name. She might eventually become accustomed to calling him Russell, but somewhere in the back of her mind, he would always be Dekker to her.

And, apparently, to himself, too.

''A name change is a pretty straightforward procedure,'' Ambrose said. ''It is handled, though, in the state of residence. Were you planning to make your home here, then, in California?''

Dekker said that no, they'd be living in Oklahoma.

''Then I'll be glad to refer you to a good attorney there.''

Dekker shook his head. ''I can handle that.'' In his line of work, he knew quite a few lawyers. ''Just wanted you to point me in the right direction.''

They rode down in the elevator with Jonas, who had a limousine waiting to take him back to his offices at Bravo, Incorporated. Joleen and Dekker returned to Angel's Crest, went their separate ways, meeting again in the living room off the grand foyer when Palmer served the predinner drinks.

At ten-thirty, they said good-night to their hosts and

climbed the curving staircase. They stopped in to pick up Sam, carried him to their rooms, put him to bed.

Then Dekker said, "I'm not really tired right now. Think I'll go out for a while."

Go out where? she thought.

But she didn't ask. She didn't feel she had the right, since she had spent the better part of the past few days trying to figure out ways to avoid him. What could she offer him right now, anyway, if he stayed here with her? Good company?

Hardly. All the old easiness between them was gone—burned away, it felt to her, by the heat of her unspoken desire.

She thought of Stacey, who had pretty much gone off the deep end over Dekker. The poor man. When women fell for him, it really messed up his life. His first wife had made him into her obsession. And now his best-friend-turned-second-wife wanted him so much she didn't dare let herself even talk to him.

"All right," she said. "Good night, then."

He gave her a brief nod in response and then he was gone. She got ready for bed and slipped between the covers.

She must have been asleep when he came in, because she had no idea what time that was.

The next day at four, in a big meeting room at the offices of Bravo, Incorporated, in downtown Los Angeles, they held the press conference.

Joleen and Dekker sat at a long table together, holding hands—Jonas had advised that—and sharing a microphone, which Jonas had suggested, as well. He said people naturally tended to be nervous in the glare of the lights, under the eyes of so many prying news people. They drew into themselves.

"If you use one mike, you'll have to sit close together. You'll be turned toward each other, leaning in. Body language sends a powerful message and we want yours to have 'happy newlyweds' written all over it."

Jonas sat on Dekker's left, with his own microphone, ready to jump in if things got too rough.

Dekker gave a short speech about how much it meant to him to have found his real family at last. Then he explained that he'd grown up next door to Joleen, in Oklahoma City. They'd been friends all their lives. And recently they'd realized that they both wanted it to be more. They had married four days ago. He also said he had a stepson named Sam, the "greatest little guy in the world."

He said he couldn't be happier, leaning toward her as he said it, to speak into the mike, holding her hand as his brother had advised him to do. His hand was warm, enclosing hers. Hers felt small. And cold at first. It warmed, though, wrapped in his. She stared at his mouth as he spoke, at the cleft in his chin, thought about all the years she had known him—her whole life. For Joleen, there had never been a world that didn't have Dekker in it.

Her throat closed up, right there, in front of all those news-hungry reporters, while Dekker said how happy he was and she stared at the cleft in his chin. She felt an insistent pressure behind her eyes....

She could have slapped her own self right smack in the face. She *never* cried. She couldn't afford to. In her family, *someone* had to keep her head at all times.

Dekker finished speaking. Then came the questions,

fast and furious, all the reporters vying to get Dekker's attention. Some of the questions were awful. Dekker handled them with a steady voice and a direct stare.

"How does it feel to be raised by your own kidnapper?"

"I didn't know she was my kidnapper. I believed she was my natural mother. She treated me well—better than well. The woman pretty much dedicated her life to raising me."

"We understand that Lorraine Smith is dead. What would you say to her, if she were still alive today?"

"She's not alive today, so I guess I don't have to figure out what to say to her."

"Your first wife died tragically, didn't she? I wonder if—"

"My first wife is not why we're here today. Next question."

At the end, the press wanted more details of the honeymoon. Were the bride and groom going anywhere else on their wedding trip, after their stay at the fabulous Angel's Crest?

Dekker answered that one with an outright lie. "No, we'll spend our entire honeymoon here in Los Angeles. We're enjoying our visit with my brother and his wife."

Joleen couldn't blame him for lying. No doubt the news people would eventually track the famous Bravo Baby down wherever he might go. But why draw them a map?

Then again, she thought, maybe it wasn't a lie. Last week Dekker had mentioned spending the second half of their honeymoon in Hawaii. But since then, he hadn't said anything about where they would go next.

Maybe in the last few discouraging days he'd decided they might as well just stay in Los Angeles until it was time to go home.

And maybe he was right. Here, the distance and the silence between them was almost bearable. They had Emma and Jonas to distract them. Sam had Mandy to play with and the nanny to look after him whenever Joleen wanted a break from the full-time job of caring for a toddler.

It would have been fun, before, just the three of them. Building sand castles on some silvery beach, catering to Sam—and just being together, talking easily about anything and everything the way they always used to do.

But now? No. Not much fun at all. Not with this silence yawning between them. Not with the secret she wouldn't share. Not with her impossible yearning eating her up every time she looked at him....

"It went well," Jonas said, after the press conference was over. "Very well. You have the knack for handling yourself in the spotlight, Dek."

"It's a knack I wouldn't mind never using again."

That night, when they went to their rooms, Dekker said he was going out again.

She longed to ask, *Where will you go? What will you do? When will you be back?*

But she kept all the questions locked up inside. She knew if she asked them, she would only be opening the door for him to ask questions of her. She still was not ready for that.

"Well, good night then...."

"Yeah. Good night, Jo...."

* * *

Dekker went outside by a set of stairs that led down to the huge back patio. As he emerged from the stairwell and shut the door behind him, he spotted one of Jonas's bodyguards, in the shadows beneath a palm tree about ten yards away.

Dekker waved. The guard raised a black-gloved hand in response.

That's me, Dekker found himself thinking, as he watched that shadowed hand saluting him through the darkness. That's me. Just two weeks ago.

So strange. His life now. It was as if he had crossed some invisible line. Gone over to the other side.

Before his brother had found him, Dekker was often the one standing in the shadows, peering in on the lives of others. Watching. And sometimes watching *over*. He'd taken a bodyguard assignment or two in the couple of years since he'd set up his agency.

Dekker strode aimlessly across the patio, to the edge of the cobalt-blue pool. He stared out over the lights of the city, the ocean beyond.

But he wasn't really seeing them. He was thinking. Thinking that now everything had changed. Now he was the Bravo Baby. The Bravo Baby all grown-up.

Someone worth watching. By reporters and syndicated press photographers. By his brother's bodyguards.

By Atwood's detectives hired to get the dirt on Jo. Jo...

How did that happen? What was she doing, creeping into his mind now?

He'd come out here, after all, to get away from her. From her silence. From the thing she couldn't make herself tell him. The thing that had no substance yet stood, impenetrable as a thick plate of shatterproof glass, between them.

He sat down on the edge of the blue, blue pool, peeled off his socks, slipped off his shoes, rolled up his trouser cuffs and dangled his legs in the water. It felt good, warm and satiny, against his skin.

He heard footsteps behind him, recognized the quiet, firm tread.

He turned. "Jonas."

His brother had changed clothes since they all went upstairs. He wore loose cotton slacks and a light shirt, unbuttoned. He was barefoot. He dropped down next to Dekker, rolled up his slacks and swung his feet into the water.

Dekker glanced back over his shoulder—at the terrace of the master suite. From that terrace, anyone sitting at the edge of the pool would be in plain view. "Been watching me, big brother?"

Jonas chuckled. "You were down here last night, too." He let a moment elapse, then asked carefully, "Anything…the matter?"

"Yeah. But I don't want to talk about it."

"Sure?"

"Positive. But thanks."

"If you change your mind…" Jonas let the thought trail off, which was fine with Dekker. He got the message, and he appreciated the offer.

Not that he'd be taking his brother up on it.

They sat for a while, feet in the water. Dekker became more aware of the city noises, distant but ever-present: the faint wailing of sirens, the whoosh of traffic so constant it sounded like the faraway roar of a waterfall. A smell of smoke hung in the air, barely detectable, but definitely there.

Finally Jonas suggested, "How about a couple of games of eight ball?" There was a pool table in the game room, on the first floor of the huge house behind them, right next-door to the media room.

Dekker shook his head. "Go on back to Emma. Get some sleep. I know you have to work tomorrow."

"You are no fun at all."

"Go on. Get lost."

Jonas pulled his feet from the water, rolled down his pants legs and stood. "There ought to be something profound I could say before I go."

Dekker looked up at his brother, watched the pool lights play on the face so much like his own. "Not necessary."

"When I was six, before our evil uncle messed everything up, there were so damn many things I was going to do for you, say to you, *teach* you. And look what happened? You went and grew up without my help."

Dekker felt himself smiling. "I guess it's a major responsibility, huh? Being a big brother."

"Words like *'daunting'* come to mind. At six I was ready. Now, well…"

"You're doing great. I mean that."

"Sure you won't let me beat you at pool?"

"I said get lost. I meant that, too."

Dekker watched his brother until he disappeared through one of the French doors that opened onto the loggia. Then he turned back to his somber contemplation of the city lights spread out below.

* * *

The next morning at breakfast Emma had an announcement to make. "Jonas and I have finally decided on the perfect wedding present for you two."

Dekker set down his fork. "Wait a minute. You've given us our present. This visit. It's a thousand times more than enough."

Emma shook a finger at him. "No, it is not. There is more. And you are getting it."

"Sounds like a threat."

"It is a visit to heaven."

"Heaven?" Joleen asked with a laugh that Dekker read instantly as faked. "Did you say—"

"You bet I did."

"Emma," said Jonas. "I think you'd better explain a little further."

"Well, all right. I will." She beamed first at Dekker and then at Joleen. "You two are leaving Friday for La Puerta al Cielo—that's Doorway to Heaven and it is a five-star resort Jonas owns, right at the tip of the Baja Peninsula. And did you notice I said 'you two'?"

Dekker nodded. Joleen was quiet. He glanced her way and noted with a tightening in his gut that apprehension had drawn a line between her brows.

Emma chattered happily on. "I said 'you two' because Sammy will stay here, with us. You will never be more than a quick flight away, if he needs you. And the two of you will get to do what newlyweds are supposed to do—spend seven long, lazy days and beautiful balmy nights with only each other to think about."

Chapter Thirteen

"What are we going to do now?"

Joleen asked the question in a low, tight voice. It was sometime later. Jonas and Emma had left for the day, and the nanny had taken the children back upstairs.

Dekker set down his coffee cup without drinking from it. It seemed crystal clear to him what they would do now. "We're going to Baja."

"But we can't just—"

"Why not? They're all supposed to think we're happy newlyweds, remember? And this is the kind of trip happy newlyweds would jump at."

She looked away. "Well, I…I think I'll have to tell Emma that though there is nothing I would love more than a week alone with my new husband, we just are not going to be able to go."

"Why not?"

She coughed, nervously, into her fist. "I'll say that I don't think I can leave Sam for all that time."

"You'll *say* that."

"Yes. I will."

"You'll *say* it, but it's not the truth, not the real reason you don't want to go away with me."

That gave her pause—though not for long. After a moment or two of heated silence, she said carefully, "Sam is only a year and a half old, and it makes perfect sense that I wouldn't want to go away for a whole week without him." She was watching him sideways, as if she didn't quite dare to look him square in the eye.

He dared. He stared at her dead-on. He was so damn sick of whatever had gone wrong with her, whatever had made her stop wanting to be with him, to talk to him. He hated this, whatever it was.

And he wanted it gone.

He said, "So it makes perfect sense. Fine. That doesn't mean it's true."

"Dekker, I don't think it matters what—"

"Let me ask you directly. If you said that you couldn't make yourself leave Sam here for a week, would it be true?"

"What does it—"

"So it would be a lie, wouldn't it? Because Sam would do just fine without you for a week. He's a well-adjusted kid. You said it yourself—zero separation anxieties. And he's made himself at home here. He likes the nanny and he likes playing with Mandy. And he will be safe. You know it. Safe from harm. Safe from that SOB grandfather of his. Because if there's anyplace in the world that no one could touch him, it's right here at Angel's Crest.''

She started to speak. He went on before she could get anything out. ''On the other hand, if he *did* have a problem, if something came up, if he got sick or whatever, we could be back here in a matter of hours.''

''Dekker, I don't—''

He cut her off that time with a short, chopping motion of his hand. She turned to follow the direction of his gaze. A maid carrying a silver coffeepot came toward them through the archway that led to the kitchen. She brought the pot to the table, refilled their cups, scooped up a few empty dishes and then left them the way she had come.

As soon as she was gone, Dekker stood. ''Let's talk about this upstairs.''

Joleen stared up at him.

She wanted to scream—just throw back her head and let out a long, loud wail. She felt so…trapped.

Trapped. And frustrated.

And confused.

And dishonest.

And just plain terrible about herself.

She spoke in a charged whisper. ''I am fed up with worryin' about what the maid thinks. I do not *care* what the maid thinks.''

His gaze bored through her. If looks could burn, she would be nothing but cinder and ash.

''Upstairs,'' he said. ''Come with me. Now.''

He confronted her as soon as they got through the door of the room they had been forced to share.

"You've had three days," he said, shoving the door shut. "Three days to 'think it over,' three days to 'deal with it'—whatever the hell 'it' is."

She put up a hand, palm out, to keep him at bay. "Please. Can't you just wait?" She backed away from him. "Can't you just let it be, let me work this out in my own time?"

He went after her, each step slow and deliberate. "No. I can't take this anymore. There is no damn thing in the world you could say to me that I can't deal with, can't find a way to understand."

She reached the center of the room, between the bed and the sitting area, and she hovered there, emotions chasing themselves across her pale face—indecision, anger, outright misery. "I just don't... I can't—"

He didn't stop until he was right in front of her. "You don't what? You can't what?"

She wrapped her arms around herself, shook her head, her eyes too big, too sad, too hopeless. "Oh, Dekker..."

And something snapped inside him. He grabbed her by the shoulders, his fingers digging in. "What, damn it? What?"

She winced.

They both froze, staring at each other. Remorse burned through him. If he had hurt her...

He uttered her name on a ragged whisper, tried to pull her close.

"No!" She jerked away, gasped, put her hand across her mouth.

All he wanted was to reach for her again—to yank her against him, to *make* her take the comfort he needed to give her.

This was going nowhere. Better to get out.

He started to turn.

"Wait." She grabbed his arm. "Oh, wait..." She let go, with a swiftness that stunned him, as if to touch him burned her. But then she gave a small cry. "Oh, please. I hate this, too, I hate what has happened between us. I hate it as much—no, *more*—than you do. Oh, Dekker, don't go...."

He faced her. And he waited. A kind of grim acceptance had settled over him. He saw no reason to push her further for answers. Either she would tell him. Or she wouldn't—and he would turn around once more and this time he *would* leave.

Her face, so pale a moment before, flooded with color. "I...can I ask you...?"

"Anything." It came out a growl. "You know that."

"The other night. Friday, our weddin' night?"

"Yeah?"

"When you—" she hesitated, swallowed, as if the next word almost choked her trying to get out "—kissed me. At the table, in front of the window, when we thought a reporter was—"

"I remember, Jo."

"Okay. Well, Dekker, um...you..." She ran out of words, lost her courage again.

He couldn't stop himself from prompting, "I...?"

"Well, you—" She sucked in a long breath and let it out in a rush. "I felt your tongue, Dekker. You used your tongue. A little. You did."

He thought he understood then. He felt like a worm. "It was a sleazy move, huh? God. I am so sorry. You probably think I'm putting the moves on you, taking advantage of our situation to—''

''No. Wait.''

''What?''

''Please. Don't be sorry.''

''Huh?''

''I do *not* think that you are putting any moves on me.''

''You don't?''

She shook her head. Her soft cheeks were the deepest pink he had ever seen them. ''I just…I want to know, um, why you did that?''

He was completely in the dark all over again. ''Wait a minute. For three days you've hardly spoken to me…because you wanted to know why I used my tongue when I kissed you…and you were too embarrassed to ask?''

She clasped her hands in front of her and stared down at them as if she were trying to see through to the bones. ''No. No, that's not it.''

''Then *what?*''

She lifted her head, cried, ''Oh, I am getting there. I am *trying* to get there. If you would just—''

He patted the air between them, palms out. ''Okay. Sorry. Take your time. It's okay…''

''I…''

''Yeah?''

''I just want to know why you did it. That's all I'm asking right now.''

''Why I…used my tongue when I kissed you?''

''Yes. Exactly. Why?''

He studied her face for an endless moment as he realized he didn't have the faintest idea. ''I, uh…''

"Yeah?"

"I wanted the kiss to look convincing to the guy outside the window. I did what I had to do to make it that way." Hadn't he?

"But your *back* was to the window. Whoever was out there couldn't tell if there were...tongues involved, or not."

He wondered, vaguely, if he'd ever had such a strange conversation as this in his life. "Hell, Jo. It seemed natural, I guess. A natural thing to do, in that situation."

"Natural?"

"Yeah. We were playing our parts, right? The bride and groom on their wedding night."

"But you never, I mean, all these years we have known each other. All my life..."

"Yeah?"

"You never did anything like that with me before."

"Right. I didn't. And I apologize. I went too far and I—"

"Don't apologize. *Please.*"

"But I—"

"Did you like it?" The words came out in a rush. Her astonished expression said it all. She couldn't believe she had said such a thing.

He quelled the sudden urge to grin. "Well, yeah."

She was frowning—a very intense sort of frown. "Are you sure you understood the question? I asked if you liked—"

"I got it. You asked if I liked kissing you, with a little bit of tongue involved." Her face, if possible, got even redder than it was already. "And I said yeah."

"It was enjoyable for you, kissing me that way?"

"Didn't I just say that?"

"Yes, I thought you did. I wanted to be sure."

"Okay, then. You can be sure."

She unclasped her hands, looked at her palms as if she couldn't decide what to do with them next. Then she whirled away, strode to the bed and dropped to the edge of it.

He approached cautiously. "Mind if I...?"

"Of course I don't. Sit."

He sat. Beside her.

"Dekker..."

He made a low noise, to let her know he was there, and that he was listening.

"Something has...happened to me. Something I never expected. Something I never *imagined*..." She looked down at her feet and added in a tiny voice, "Or at least, I don't *think* I imagined." She let out a tiny groan. "Oh, I don't know. I don't know if I can bear to tell you...to ask you..." She shook her head slowly, wearily, back and forth.

He waited. What else could he do at that point? Maybe Atwood had somehow managed to get through the extensive security network his brother employed at Angel's Crest, managed to get through and threaten her somehow. Maybe she had some incurable disease.

It didn't matter. Whatever it was, as soon as she told him, they could face it together.

"I don't know how to say it," she murmured. "Except to just *say* it..."

"Good idea."

She drew herself up and looked straight at him. He had never seen her look so determined—or so lost.

She said, "Dekker, I...I *want* you. I know this is a lot to ask, but do you think, maybe, that we could make love together?"

Chapter Fourteen

It was not what he'd expected. Not by a long shot.

And he must have looked as thunderstruck as he felt, because she instantly jumped to her feet and started protesting. "Oh. Oh, look. Never mind." She threw up both hands. "Oh, why did I say that? I do not believe that I said that." She pressed her hands against her ears, as if by blocking out sound she could somehow take back the words.

Then she dropped her hands to her sides, heaved a big sigh and pleaded, "Oh, Dekker. Could we…do you think we could, um, pretend that I never said that?"

"Jo…"

"No. Now, you listen."

He looked at her levelly.

"Are you listening?"

He nodded, to show that he was.

And she asked again, "Will you *please* forget what I just said?"

She had to know the answer to that one. He said nothing, just went on looking her square in the eye.

A shudder passed through her. "Oh. Oh, this is awful. I never should have told you. You should have let me just—"

"Jo. Settle down. *Sit* down. Please."

She chewed on her lower lip for a moment, her sweet face contorted with distress. And then, with a little moan, she slumped back down beside him.

He gave her—and himself—a moment to regroup. Then, with some caution, he put his arm around her.

She let out a second small, agonized groan. He held on to her—but lightly. After another iffy moment, she relaxed and laid her head on his shoulder.

"Jo," he said softly. "This is not a terrible thing."

"Oh, well," she mumbled. "Easy for you to say."

He kissed the top of her head, gave her shoulder a squeeze. "We've been through so much together. We can get through this."

She gave a small humph. "How?"

Now she'd finally told him what she wanted, it all seemed very clear to him. Simple as adding one and one and coming up with two. "If you want this marriage to have sex in it, well, okay. That's fine with me."

She gave him a nudge with her elbow in the old, wonderful, teasing way. "Don't get too excited at the idea."

"I'm excited." And he was, suddenly—that hot, rising feeling.

She must have been looking down at his lap, because her head shot up. "Dekker!"

He spoke lazily, with some humor. "Well now, Jo. If lovemaking's in the offing, a man will often become excited."

"Oh, really? Thanks for the tip."

"Anytime."

She looked…what? Doubtful? Concerned? He suggested tenderly, "Go ahead. Say it. Whatever it is."

"I just…I wasn't sure. I didn't know. If you would want to, with me. If you even *could*."

Even with all her hesitations and sighs, he took her meaning. "There was a while there, a few years ago, when I couldn't. But recently, I have noticed that the necessary equipment has started showing signs of life again."

She looked at him expectantly. And he decided that it was about time they went ahead and got it out there, said the name. Told the truth. "You heard about the problem from Stacey, right?"

Jo nodded.

"What did she tell you?"

"Oh, vague things. She never said it outright. But she hinted, once or twice, in the last few months you were still living together, that you were not able to, uh…"

"Get it up?"

She lifted one shoulder in a half-shrug. "I didn't take her too seriously. She said so many crazy things at the end. It got so I could never tell what she'd made up in her own confused, unhappy mind, and what had really happened. I learned that whatever she said, I shouldn't put a lot of store in it—but then, the night of DeDe's weddin', when you and I were talking about man-woman love…?'' She let the sentence wander off, looked at him for confirmation.

He gave it. ''Yeah, I remember.''

''Dead meat, is what you said. That you were dead meat when it came to man-woman love.''

''That's right, I said that—and?''

''Well, it kind of stuck with me. And later, after you kissed me at my house on our own weddin' night, after I started realizing that I would like it if you kissed me some more, I did get to wondering if maybe what Stacey said had been true.''

''It was. I couldn't do it, couldn't make love with her, not there at the end. Maybe I still did love her, even then. It's hard to say. But I sure as hell didn't *want* her. I didn't even *want* to want her.''

''Oh, Dekker. I am so sorry….''

He lifted his hand from her shoulder, laid it against her silky hair, felt the warmth of it, the tender curve of her skull beneath his palm. ''There is no reason for you to be sorry.''

''You never would have met her, if she hadn't been my friend.''

''That hardly makes my bad marriage your fault.''

''I wanted…to help you. To help *both* of you. I loved you both, so much, and you were both so unhappy, both hurting so bad.''

''You did help.'' He clasped her shoulder again, gave it a squeeze. ''You saved my damn life, after Stacey was gone. And you did all you could to help her, too. More than *I* ever did, that's for sure.''

''No. I didn't.''

''Yes, you did.''

"It wasn't enough."

"Jo. With Stacey, nothing was *ever* enough."

She let out a small, mournful sound. "So sad…"

"Yeah. Yeah, it was. Real sad…" He insinuated his hand beneath the warm, silky fall of her hair. She lifted her head from his shoulder and looked at him, mouth tipped up, dark eyes alight.

He wrapped his hand around the back of her neck. So good, he thought. To be able to touch her again. To let himself touch her in this whole new way. He brushed her lips lightly with his, felt her shiver slightly, beneath his hand.

It came to him that he loved the scent of her, that he always had and always would. She smelled of soap and shampoo. Clean. Fresh. With that tempting hint of flowers—and something more. Something that was distinctly Jo, something that, to him, would always mean all the good things, the sweetest things….

"Dekker?"

"Um?"

"Do you want to…right now?"

"Do you?"

"Oh, yes." Her eagerness enchanted him. But then she frowned. "I, well, I think it is only fair to warn you. I'm not all that experienced. It was only a few times, with Bobby. And I have to admit, those times weren't very good. I always thought that it *could* be, you know, good. But I didn't know what I was doin', and Bobby Atwood was…well, for a guy goin' nowhere, he was sure in an all-fired hurry to get there, if you know what I mean."

He kissed the end of her nose. "We'll work it out."

"I just wanted you to know."

He put his mouth on hers again, tasting. She sighed some more, her lips softly parting, inviting his tongue inside.

He could never have refused such a sweet invitation.

He tasted her, more deeply, sweeping the secret flesh of her underlip, running his tongue over her pretty white teeth, and then meeting *her* tongue, which shyly darted back at first, then, hesitant but eager, came forward to rub against his own.

He guided her back, to lie across the bed with him. She went without hesitation, smiling against his mouth.

They lay there, kissing—long, lazy kisses. He was enjoying every sigh, every slightest hungry quiver of her body under his. He wanted to make it last, stretch it out into forever. To make it last for her sake, because she was Jo, because that fool, Atwood, hadn't had sense enough to love her the way she ought to be loved.

For her sake, and also for his own.

This, now—Jo's mouth under his, her sweet, soft body moving beneath his hands—this was a gift the likes of which he had never thought to know.

So damn many gifts she had given him, down all the years. Gifts of loyalty, gifts of time, the simple gift of her presence when he had been hopelessly lost and completely alone, when he had nothing to say and nothing left inside himself to give to anyone else. The gift of her insistence, her refusal to give up on him, that dogged stubbornness in her that made her stick with a friend till the end, no matter what.

So damn many gifts.

And now this…

He wanted to make it good for her, to show her what it *could* be, between a woman and a man, so that later, when the threat Robert Atwood posed to her had been effectively neutralized, when she was ready to move on to the kind of man she deserved, she'd go with confidence in herself as a desirable woman, with the full knowledge of how to take pleasure and how to give it back in kind.

He raised his head enough that he could look at her, at her flushed face, her kiss-swollen mouth. Her lashes fluttered up and her eyes were so dark and soft right then, he thought of summer nights or of falling, falling forever, but into a good place.

She asked his name, on a whisper of breath, and she raised a hand, brushed it lightly back from his temple, fingers stroking his hair, sliding against his scalp in a tender brand and then gone.

He lowered his mouth to the smooth space between her brows, murmured, "What?" against her skin.

But she had no real question, or if she did, it had already become unnecessary to ask it. Because she only closed her eyes again, stroked his shoulder, said his name once more, so low, on a moan.

He touched the side of her throat, felt the pounding of her pulse there. And then he pressed his mouth where his fingers had been, taking a long, lazy moment to taste the rhythm of her heart, smiling to himself when she sucked in a little gasp at the feel of his tongue on her skin.

Tenderly, still feeding on the pulse point in her throat, he let his fingers wander downward—but not too far. Just enough to cup his hand over one soft, upthrusting breast. She gasped again.

He raised his head and waited for her to look at him. Those lashes fluttered up. She gave him a smile— one that trembled at first and then bloomed wide.

He found he was as hungry to look as to touch. So he let his gaze wander down the curvy length of her, gently molding her breast at the same time, feeling the nipple pressing into his palm even through the layers of cloth that protected it.

She wore a T-shirt the color of a mango when you cut it open, exposing the sweet meat inside. And a pair of trim green slacks that came midway between her knees and her ankles. Slip-on sandals on her feet.

She lifted her head to see what he was looking at.

He suggested, his voice gruff with arousal, ''You could get rid of those sandals with no effort at all.''

As he watched, she toed off one sandal and then the other. They thumped to the rug at the side of the bed.

''How's that?'' she asked, a little breathless.

He looked into her face again, saw excitement and the glint of apprehension. ''Perfect.'' He touched her mouth, with the pads of two fingers, then traced those fingers downward, putting his own mouth where his fingers had been, kissing her again, feeding on her mouth, drawing on her tongue until she surrendered it, gave it up, let him have it to suck on.

She moaned, and another of those long, hungry shivers went through her. He felt that shiver under his hands as it shimmered down her body.

Her body...

Strange. He'd known her virtually her entire life, remembered standing over her crib a few days after her birth, amazed at how ugly a baby could be, thinking that something so small and unappealing would need to be protected, knowing, even then, at the age of five, that he would always protect her, no matter what.

But her body?

Until lately it hadn't concerned him much. Oh, as she'd grown-up, he'd been well aware that she wasn't the least bit ugly anymore, that she had all the right curves in all the right places. But her curviness, her womanliness, didn't seem to have anything at all to do with him or with their relationship to each other.

Until lately…

Lately—as in that dress the other night, the one that wasn't quite gold and wasn't quite brown, the one that hugged all those curves that weren't supposed to concern him. Yeah, he could still picture it, the way that dress had clung to her backside when she'd turned and walked away from him.

And in that swimsuit she'd found in the cabana that same day—it was turquoise and blue, with splashes of gold at the waist. She had stretched out on that rubber raft and floated there so peacefully. He'd known she'd wanted to be left alone, and he'd known he ought to let her have what she wanted. But he hadn't been able to resist the desire to get close to her. Eventually he had surfaced at her side.

At first she wouldn't look at him. She lay with her cheek on her arm, her head turned away.

Since she wouldn't look at him, he let himself look at her.

At her body.

The word ''smooth'' had come to mind. Smooth

and soft. Warm. Touchable. Tiny hairs glinted like gold dust on the backs of her thighs.

He'd thought then that he did want to touch her—feel the warmth, the smoothness, the silkiness of those little hairs....

He wanted to touch her. And in much more than just a friendly way. He'd felt his body rising, responding to the sight of the woman that he wanted.

And it was okay to let himself want her. It was good to know that he *could* want a woman again—after all, for a while, there had been some doubt on that score.

Also, he had been certain, there in the pool, that he would never do anything about wanting her. They were friends, married for a time, because she needed to be married. But she herself had defined the terms, that night in her mother's backyard.

We are deep and true friends. But we are not lovers....

He'd dribbled that water over her thighs to force her to look at him—and also to watch the way it beaded up and glittered as it trickled over her skin....

"Dekker?" She was staring up at him now, stretched out with him across this bed he had never thought to share with her. He saw a hundred questions in her eyes.

For the first time as a man with her, he felt more than aroused. He felt...something hot and insistent, something very close to need.

He sucked in a long breath and thought about control—that he needed to exercise a little of it about now. He couldn't really have her now, be inside her, feel her softness closing around him. He would have to wait for that. This marriage of theirs was not forever.

They couldn't afford to go making any babies together. And at the moment he had nothing to keep a baby from happening.

Then again, maybe she did. It was doubtful. But no harm in asking.

"Are you on the pill, Jo?"

Those eyes went wide again. She shook her head. "Oh, I didn't even think about that."

He smoothed his hand down her hair again, wrapped a coil of the silky stuff around a finger. "No diaphragm handy, huh?"

"Uh-uh." She started to sit up.

He clasped her shoulder. "Where are you going?"

"Uh, well, I thought, you know, that we'd have to wait until—"

"Please stay here. For a little."

"But we probably shouldn't—"

"We won't. Not until later. Not until tonight."

She swallowed. "Tonight?"

He nodded, thinking of what they *could* do now, that he could still give her pleasure, maybe get to see her face as a climax shuddered through her, certainly get to see her naked, here, in the warm light of a California morning.

The mango-colored shirt ended at her waist. Such a simple act, to insinuate his hand between it and the satiny skin of her belly. He pushed the shirt up, put his mouth there, on her stomach, swirled his tongue around her navel, then dipped it into that tender little groove.

"Oh!" she said, and "Oh!" again.

He pushed the shirt up farther. "Raise your arms." She did. He pulled the shirt over her head and then tossed it toward a chair a few feet from the bed. Her bra was bright pink, and her breasts swelled temptingly from the lacy cups. The thing hooked in the back, though.

He'd deal with it in a minute. He slid a finger under the button at the waist of the green slacks.

"Dekker Smith, what are you up to?"

"That's *Bravo,* or it will be soon." With a flick of his thumb, the button came undone.

She let out a small sound of distress as he tugged her zipper down. "Well all right then. Dekker Bravo, you are undressing me."

"That's right. Lift up."

"But you said that we—"

He put a finger to her lips. "Shh. Trust me?"

She gently pushed his hand away. "You know that I do."

"We'll be careful."

"Isn't that what men and women are always saying to each other, right before they get carried away and end up not being careful at all?"

"Maybe it is. But this is different. We're not kids. I have…some measure of control. I won't go any farther than we can afford to go. I promise you."

She looked at him, long and deep. "You're sure?"

Was he? Hell, yes. He was sure. He could do this. Touch. Taste. But not possess. "Positive."

"We're just going to…?"

"Play a little. Safe play. I promise. Later I'll go out and get us some protection. And then, tonight…" He let the thought finish itself.

"Hmm," she said, a pleased sort of sound, and then she put her soft hand on the side of his face. "Well, anyway. If something did happen now, we *are* married...."

"Nothing's going to happen," he vowed. "Nothing that will make babies. I swear it."

Her eyes probed his for another long moment. Then she said the word he was waiting for. "Okay."

It was all he needed to hear. He put his mouth back on hers and he kissed her, another endless, seeking, very wet kiss. As he kissed her, he undressed her, pushing those green pants off her hips and down, getting rid of her silky panties. And then, finally, taking away her bra.

She sighed and she moaned, and she pressed herself close to him, those beautiful bare breasts against his chest, her legs rubbing along his. He began kissing his way down her body, tasting her flesh, finding it so sweet and tender, so warm. So good...

He lingered at her breasts for a long time, sucking the hard little nipples into his mouth, rolling his tongue around them, loving the way she lifted her body, pressing it closer, giving him more....

He moved lower, down over her soft belly, to the nest of brown curls at the top of her thighs. By then all her initial apprehension had fled. She was openly, honestly needful, clutching his shoulders, making hungry, willing noises deep in her throat.

He loved that. Her very openness. She was just so...responsible, as a rule. Letting go rarely came easily to her.

Gently, he pushed her thighs apart and settled between them. She stiffened and she gasped when he put his mouth on her. And then she cried out.

And after that cry, she surrendered completely,

opening wider, offering herself up to him, letting him do what he wanted, letting him taste her so deeply, he would never forget, never lose her completely. Always, in the most primal part of his consciousness, the taste of her would linger, imprinted on his senses, a branding on his soul.

She was wet and slick, dripping with her need and his hunger combined. She held his head, slim fingers splayed, gripping hard, pushing her body frantically against him. He held on, too, cradling her bottom in his hands, lifting her up like a cup to drink from, running his tongue over the soft, secret folds, latching on and sucking deeply, rubbing the swollen nub of flesh that was the center of her pleasure.

She said things, promised things, wild things. Things like forever. He took those promises for what they were: words of the moment, of her passion.

They did not have forever. But they did have right now.

And now was good enough—more than good enough. It was better than anything he'd ever expected. A gift. The perfect kind of gift—given so freely and completely unsought. A gift he would save in his heart, even after he had to let her go.

The tiny, soft explosions started. He felt them, there, against his tongue.

He stayed with her, maintaining the secret, intimate kiss as the long shudders took her. She cried out again. And again. He held on, his mouth tight against her, tasting her woman's release, sharing her pleasure at its highest point, until she went lax with a heavy sigh and pushed at his shoulders.

"Oh. Stop...I can't..." He took pity on her then

and broke the long, forbidden kiss. "Oh, come up here. Up here, to me…" Her hands weren't pushing anymore. They were pulling, tugging, urging him upward. He went to her, moved up her body. She wrapped those soft arms around him, and she buried her head against his neck.

"Oh," she said again. And then his name, over and over, a litany, a soft, tender chant. "Dekker, Dekker, Dekker, Dekker…"

He made a low, rough, questioning sound.

She chuckled. It was the naughtiest laugh he had ever heard. "What you did…I do not believe what you did…"

He smoothed her hair and he stroked her slim back and he held on, tight. She slid her leg between his, rubbing her body up close, as if she would melt right into him. When she got where she wanted to be, she went still.

They lay like that for a time, arms and legs entwined.

She was the one who moved first. She reached down between them and cupped her hand over his fly.

Molten heat went pouring through him. He pulled back enough to give her a warning look. "Better not."

Those big dark eyes gleamed at him. "Trust me." She stuck out that pink tongue of hers and moistened those soft, tempting lips. "Nothing's going to happen that will make babies. I swear it."

What else could he do?

He whispered, "Okay."

Chapter Fifteen

The too-brief days that followed were magical, the nights pure enchantment. They were the kind of nights Joleen had never dared to imagine she might someday know.

They kept their word to each other, that first morning, played with each other, did the most shocking and incredible things to each other—but held back from making love fully.

In the afternoon Dekker went out and got what they needed.

And that night they were careful and quiet, with Sam so close, right in the next room. They engaged the privacy lock on his door and they held their hands over each other's mouths when one or the other got too carried away.

Carried away…

Oh, yes. That was the word for it.

Dekker plain and simply carried her away.

He kissed her and caressed her until her body felt as if all the nerves had been swollen, turned inside out, so that even the feel of the air on her skin was almost too pleasurable to bear. And when he came into her...oh, was there ever any feeling quite like that?

To hold him inside her, pushing in her so deep, reaching for the very center of her, surging toward her heart.

How could it be? *Dekker,* of all people. Here she'd grown-up right next door to him and never known the things that he would someday do to her body, the wonder he would bring to her, the sweet, shattering spell he would weave on her senses.

Could they go on like this forever? Oh, probably not. But that was okay. Just to have this, for now, was more pure magic than Joleen ever would have asked of life.

Sammy put up no fuss at all when they left for the resort on Friday morning. He let Joleen kiss him good-bye and then he squirmed to get down.

"Pway, Mama. Manny..." He had Mandy's name by then, but without the *d.*

"He will be right here, *señora,*" the nanny promised. "I will take very, very good care."

Dekker took her hand. "Come on, Jo. The car is waiting...."

La Puerta al Cielo. Doorway to heaven.

And it was. The resort consisted of a spacious open-air lobby overlooking seven sugar-cube white buildings, two suites in each. On the grounds and near the buildings prickly flowering cactus, ironwood and palo verde trees grew. Gleaming little brooks, accented with miniature waterfalls, wound in and out among the desert blooms.

Doorway to heaven. Oh, definitely.

Their suite was twice the size of Joleen's house. The talavera-tiled bathroom contained a tub every bit as roomy as the one they'd left behind at Angel's Crest, a tub made for lovers. And the bathroom and the bedroom kind of blended together, so a person could step right through from bath to bed. Joleen and Dekker found this feature wonderfully convenient.

Even the floors of the place took a person's breath away. They were made of fossilized limestone from Yucatan, one of the attendants explained, inset with pebbles in intricate designs. *Tapates de piedras,* the attendant called them: "stone carpets," mosaic designs of fish and birds that made Joleen think of exotic and faraway places—Ancient Greece or maybe Rome.

They had an ocean-view patio, furnished with big white-cushioned rattan chairs, with a telescope in case they felt the urge to gaze more closely at the stars. There was a half-moon-shaped hot tube built into the patio wall, and a set of stairs that spiraled upward to the roof.

And there was a bed on that roof. The first night of their visit, very late, they climbed those stairs and used that bed. It was more than the doorway to heaven that night. Lying there on the rooftop patio, with Dekker— *joined* with Dekker—that was heaven itself. The velvet night so warm and sweet around them, and the stars so close she felt she could reach out and grab a handful, cool silver light to carry with her when they went back downstairs.

He pressed so deep into her, and then withdrew, and then, slowly, filled her again. She sighed and moved with him, accepting him, losing him, calling him back to her once more. She thought of the ocean, sliding up on the shore, ebbing away, only to return again, over and over, the rhythm endless. And endlessly sweet...

The next day, near twilight, they walked on the beach, which was gold as the pelt of a lion, the sand so fine, silky as bath powder. They watched the evening light soften, watched the sky turn pink and then the sea. Slowly, magically, it all deepened to indigo as the night came on.

Then they went back to their suite and they made love some more.

The days seemed to flow, one into the other. Two days. Three. Four. Five...

Except for missing Sam, she could go on like this forever.

But time did not stand still for them. Friday came. They flew back to Los Angeles. Sam ran to her when she went to him in the nursery. He clung to her.

For about five minutes.

Then he was squirming to get down, calling for "Manny."

They stayed the weekend with Emma and Jonas, spending lots of time with the children, in the nursery and out by the pool. Then, when the nights came, heaven was waiting all over again.

Monday they boarded one of Jonas's jets and took

off for home. Joleen felt a little sad to leave the magic of their honeymoon behind.

But there was so much to do, their whole lives to live. They would start looking for a house immediately, and Joleen would have to find the right day care, and of course things would be hectic at the salon. She'd have a lot of catching up to do, after two weeks away.

And Dekker had started talking about expanding his detective business. He wanted to find a bigger, nicer office in a better building than he was in now. He'd hire some office help, start looking for a couple more good investigators.

"What I'm talking about," he said, "is starting over from the ground up." He'd been running things by the seat of his pants up till now. For their honeymoon he'd just locked everything up and made sure the answering machine was on. If he expanded, he'd have people to cover for him whenever he took time off.

It would be a whole new ball game, he said. And he seemed to be looking forward to it, to using some of the money he'd inherited and making A-1 Investigations into the biggest and best agency in the city.

There would also be the Atwoods to deal with. But that didn't worry her so much anymore. Once she found the right day care, she would be ready. Ready in every sense of the word to deflect whatever accusations Robert Atwood tried to throw at her. Especially now that she and Dekker shared a bed. Let Bobby's awful father send his detectives around to spy on them. Those detectives would see a couple who were married in every sense of the word.

The Bravo jet touched down at Will Rogers World

Airport at a little after one in the afternoon. They got all the way to Joleen's house in the Lexus without spotting a single reporter on their tail.

It had been so relaxing at Angel's Crest and in Baja. No reporters ever got past the gates at the Bravo mansion. And the exclusive resort was the same. At La Puerta al Cielo, any nosy person wanting to sneak a peak at the spectacular grounds—or at the lucky few who enjoyed such luxury—was simply turned away by the security guard at the front gate.

Now that they were back home, they'd probably have to deal with the media again, at least to some extent. But not yet. Joleen decided to enjoy the privacy while it lasted.

Joleen's little house seemed somehow to have grown even smaller after the lavish accommodations they'd enjoyed for the past couple of weeks—smaller and a little bit worn. That threadbare spot on the arm of her easy chair hadn't seemed quite so obvious to her before. And she'd never really noticed how many scars and scuffs marred the surface of her big round oak coffee table.

Still, this little house *was* home—and would be until they found a new one. She felt a rush of affection for the place. She also felt chilly. The weather had turned. The sky outside was a sheet of gray, the temperature in the forties, a misty rain falling. Dekker checked the furnace and fired it up.

Sammy had eaten on the plane and was more than ready for his nap. Joleen put him down. He was out almost the minute his little head hit the pillow. She turned from his bed to find Dekker waiting in the doorway to the dining room. She pulled the door closed as she crossed the threshold and went to him, sliding her arms around his hard waist.

She tipped her mouth up. He took it. They shared a long, slow, lovely kiss.

He was the one who broke it. "You're shivering."

"Umm. Heater's on, though. In a few minutes, I'll be just fine." She stretched up, planted another kiss on those wonderful lips of his, a quick one, that time. "Hungry?"

"Always." The corners of his mouth curved up in a lazy smile. He cupped her bottom and pulled her in tightly against him, so that she could feel just how hungry he was.

She tried to look reproachful, though her every nerve had set to humming with naughty anticipation. "You know I meant for lunch."

He bent his head and nibbled at her neck. "*I* didn't."

She tried not to moan. "I thought...didn't you say you had to get over to the agency?"

"Soon..." He breathed the word against her skin.

She felt his tongue, sliding along the skin of her throat, followed by the light scrape of his teeth. She did moan then.

He pretended she had actually said a real word. "What was that?"

"I think..."

"Yeah?"

She reached around behind her and grabbed one of the hands that held her bottom. "You had better come with me." She pulled him toward the kitchen—and the door in there that led to her bedroom.

They were passing the phone on the kitchen wall

when it jarred to life. They both jumped, froze, looked at the phone and then at each other. The phone rang again.

Joleen did not want to answer. Neither did Dekker. She could see that in his midnight eyes.

But their honeymoon was over. They were back in real life now. They had to start dealing with all the usual responsibilities again. And besides, she thought rather smugly, once they closed their bedroom door of an evening, they could head straight for heaven. And they could go there every night, with little chance of interruption.

Dekker was watching her face, reading it, she knew. He saw that she would answer the call. So he did it for her, snaring the phone off the wall in the middle of the third ring and holding it out to her.

She pressed it to her ear and heard her mother's voice. "Joly? Baby? Is that you?"

"Hi, Mama."

"How long have you been home?"

"Not long. Twenty minutes or so."

"I left a message for you to call me as soon as you got in."

"Sorry. I haven't checked my messages yet."

"Well, never mind. I have reached you. Did you have a good time?"

"I did. A wonderful time."

"And Dekker?"

Joleen hooked a finger in the belt loop of her husband's faded jeans. She gave a tug to get him up nice and close, then planted a quick kiss right on the dent in his chin. "Dekker had a fine time, too—everything okay? At the shop? At home?"

"Everything is fine. No problems. Is Dekker there with you now?"

"He sure is."

"And our Sammy?"

"We just put him down for his nap."

"Good—I want you to stay right there, both you and Dekker. Do not go anywhere."

Now, what was going on? "But Mama, what—"

"Don't start askin' questions. It will all be explained."

"You know, Mama, I hate it when you get mysterious on me."

"One hour, okay? Don't either of you go anywhere for sixty full minutes. Give me your solemn vow on that."

"Mama—"

"Joleen, I want to hear your promise."

"All right, all right. I promise. An hour."

"Dekker, too."

"But—"

"Ask him."

Joleen blew out an exasperated breath and put her hand over the receiver, "Mama wants to talk to us. I don't know what about. She says she'll be here within an hour and she wants us both to promise to wait here till she comes."

He shrugged. "Tell her we'll be here."

Joleen spoke into the receiver again. "All right. We'll be here."

"Good." The line went dead.

Joleen held the phone away from her ear and glared at it. "I hate when she does stuff like this."

Dekker chuckled. He took the phone and hooked it

back on the wall. Then he pulled Joleen close. She rested her head against his heart and grumbled, "Kind of spoiled the mood, didn't she? How can I drag you back to my room and have my way with you when Mama could be knockin' on the door any second now?"

He lifted her chin with a finger. "Buck up."

She pulled a sour face. "Isn't it nice to be home?"

"Maybe I'll take a sandwich, after all...."

So they had lunch while they waited.

Joleen got some bread from the freezer and opened a can of tuna. Dekker had a Rolling Rock and she had a Fresca over ice.

When they'd eaten the sandwiches, Joleen rinsed the dishes and put them in the dishwasher. Then she sat back down with Dekker at the table. He nursed his beer, and she ended up getting herself a second Fresca before they heard the doorbell ring.

Camilla hardly gave the bell a chance to finish chiming before she was poking her head in the door and calling out, "Hel-lo!"

Joleen and Dekker got up and started for the living room. Three steps later, as they cleared the doorway to the dining room, they saw that Camilla wasn't alone.

Antonia Atwood stood at her side—and a much different Antonia than the mouse in mauve who had attended DeDe's wedding three weeks before.

The faded brown hair had been artfully permed and colored and beautifully cut in a soft chin-length style. And the face...

Why, it was a *pretty* face now, cleverly enhanced

by a deft hand. The effect was not of a woman made up, but a woman at her best, her eyes wide and bright, her cheeks flushed with healthy color, her mouth soft and inviting and subtly red.

And Antonia's taste in clothes had changed, too. What she wore now suited her perfectly. Simple lines, the best fabrics: a silk shirt the color of a ripe peach, linen slacks in honey tan.

Joleen knew instantly who had wrought this amazing transformation. She confronted the culprit. "Mama. Tell me you are not the one. Tell me you have not had this woman over at the salon "

"Well now, baby, I can't tell you that. Because the truth is, I have. We have become real close in the last two weeks, Tony and I, and—"

"Tony?" Joleen could hardly believe her ears. "You call her *Tony* now?"

"That's right. I do. And I want you to settle down, you hear me? Don't go jumpin' to any conclusions until you understand all that has happened while you were away."

It was a reasonable request, and Joleen knew it. She commanded, in a controlled tone, "Talk, Mama. And make it good."

But Antonia was the one who spoke next. "Please," she said, her wispy voice changed somehow, sounding so much stronger, so much more sure than before. "Let's start with the most important point, with the reason that I am here, now, in your house."

That sounded like an excellent idea. "Well, fine. You tell me. Why are you here?"

"Because I want you to know that I have done what

needed doing. I have stood up to my husband for the first time in our thirty-plus years together. There will be no lawsuit. No one is going to try to take Samuel away from you.''

Chapter Sixteen

Joleen's legs had gone suddenly wobbly. "I don't...I can't believe that you—" What was she trying to say? Whatever it was, it had flown clean out of her head.

Her mother said, "Honey, you look like you could use a chair. You come on in here and sit down."

Dekker had her by the elbow. He guided her into the living room and eased her into the chair with the threadbare spot on the arm.

Once he had her settled, he frowned down at her. "What can I get you? What do you need?"

"Nothing." She reached out, touched his arm in reassurance. "I'm okay." He still looked way too concerned. She spoke with more force. "Seriously. I am fine." As she said the words, she found they were true. The shock of what she'd just heard was passing.

Dekker moved to the side, but stayed with her, next to her chair.

She sat up straighter. Her mother and Antonia Atwood stood, side by side, across the oak coffee table. It was a united front if Joleen had ever seen one.

And Camilla had the strangest expression on her face. She looked at Dekker and she glanced at Joleen and then quickly looked back at Dekker again. "Hmm," she said softly. "Oh, yes. Oh, my, yes."

Whatever her mother was mumbling about, it could wait. Joleen wanted a few answers. And she wanted them now.

"All right," she said. "I am listening. I hope that one of you plans to explain what has been happening around here."

Camilla stopped glancing back and forth between Joleen and Dekker. She cleared her throat. "Well, I suppose you could say it all started two days after you left for California."

Antonia nodded. "That was when I went to speak with your mother at the salon."

Camilla grinned. "I ordered her out, at first."

"But I was persistent."

"You certainly were." The two women shared a smile that could only be called fond.

Then Antonia looked at Joleen again. "I approached your mother because, by the time I got up my courage…by the time I finally accepted the fact that I would have to take action, that I could not allow things to go on as they were, you and your new husband had gone out of town. It was all over the newspapers, about your marriage—" she glanced up at Dekker "—and about you, Dekker, about what you'd learned of your real background." Her eyes met Joleen's again. "And Robert was furious. He had talked to our lawyer, of course, and been told that your marriage and your new husband's wealth would make things a lot harder for him. Pretty much impossible, really, was what the lawyer said…''

Antonia paused. A small sound of distress escaped her. "Oh, my dear Joleen, the whole time, even before your sister's wedding day, when Robert first told me what he planned to do, I knew it was so very, very wrong. I'd seen you with Samuel, seen with my own eyes what a fine mother you are. And I also knew…'' She hesitated, as if whatever she meant to say was just too difficult to admit.

But then she forged on. "I knew that Robert and I had not been the parents to our darling Bobby that we should have been. That Bobby had grown-up to be…weak. And irresponsible. That what he'd done to you, leaving you all on your own with a baby to raise, was unforgivable. And yet, there you were, reaching out to us, offering us a place in your little boy's life. I did admire you. So much. But Robert—'' Antonia hung her beautifully groomed head. "Oh, I don't know. I just don't know about that man.''

"Now, now, Tony.'' Camilla wrapped a comforting arm around the other woman's shoulder. "It is going to be okay, now. You know that. It will be all right.''

Antonia sent Camilla a grateful glance, then turned to Joleen again. "Oh, I wish you could understand, though of course I know I cannot expect you to. My husband could not bear to admit how totally we failed, with our son. And he would have given anything for what he will never have—another chance. He was— he still is, really—terribly confused. He convinced himself that he could somehow start all over. That it was his duty to steal your son from you and raise Samuel the way he knew, deep in his heart, that he should have raised our Bobby.'' Antonia's eyes had a faraway look, at that moment. Faraway and infinitely sad.

She seemed to shake herself. ''But that was then. Now, as I told you, there is no way he will even *try* to take Samuel away from you.''

Joleen leaned forward. ''You sound so certain about that.''

''I am. Very certain. You see, after I talked with Camilla…'' Antonia paused to fondly pat the hand that clasped her shoulder. ''I went to Robert and I told him that there would be no custody battle. That if he tried such a thing, I would not only leave him, I would be there, in court, to testify in your behalf.'' A bleak smile lifted the edges of Antonia's mouth. ''He was not happy with me. I spent two nights at your mother's house, as a matter of fact, to give him a chance to cool down a little. But we are…working on our problems now. And it looks as if we may come through this together, still married to each other, after all.

''Joleen.'' Antonia pulled away from Camilla. She took a step to the side, as if she would go on around the coffee table, come to where Joleen sat in the comfy old chair. But then she stopped herself. ''I hope someday you can bring yourself to forgive me. And maybe eventually even find it in your heart to forgive Robert, too. I should have come forward sooner. I know that. I am so sorry, not only for what my son did to you, but also for all those terrible things Robert said to you the day that your sister was married. And beyond that, for the constant anxiety you must have suffered in the past few weeks, believing you would be facing a long, drawn-out court battle. I wanted to try to call you, as soon as I'd confronted Robert..."

"But I stopped her," Camilla said, sounding thoroughly pleased with herself. "I wanted you to have that time away." A knowing gleam lit up the big brown eyes. "I can see I was right, too—that your little getaway has been very good, for both of you. And, anyway, the news was right here, waitin' for you, when you got home. Oh, it is all going to work out, now, isn't it? It is all going to work out just fine." Now those brown eyes were brimming.

Joleen said, "Mama," in a warning tone.

"I won't," vowed Camilla. "I will not start in cryin' right now. You do not have to worry. You have my word."

Joleen turned her gaze to the woman at her mother's side. More than a good haircut and a few makeup tips had happened to Antonia Atwood. A much deeper change had taken place. Here was a woman who had finally stood up for what she believed in. The quaking mauve mouse was no more.

Slow down here, a more cynical voice in the back of Joleen's mind cautioned. A little suspicion is healthy. This could be a trick, some new angle Robert Atwood has decided to try against you, a clever way to get you to let down your guard.

But Joleen didn't believe that. How could she?

Just looking in Antonia's eyes told the real story. Bobby Atwood's mother had taken a stand. And she would not be backing down from it.

Joleen said, "Thank you, for this. For doing the right thing. For...coming to me now."

Antonia dipped her chin in a nod of acknowledgment. "It's not enough. But it is a start. And I also want you to know that arrangements have been made for you to get the financial support Bobby should have provided when he learned there would be a baby. It will be a considerable amount of money. Our family lawyer will be contacting you in the next few days to discuss all the details."

Joleen opened her mouth to protest that she didn't need any money. But she shut it without speaking. It wasn't *her* money, after all. It was Sam's, and he did have a right to it.

The grandmothers left a few minutes later, after Camilla extracted a promise from Joleen that she and Dekker and Sam would have dinner at her house that night.

As soon as she let the two older women out the front door, Joleen turned to her husband. "Well. What do you think of that?"

He shrugged.

She peered at him more closely. "All of a sudden you are very quiet."

"What is there for me to say?"

Something had changed. She couldn't put her finger on what. "Is something wrong?"

"Not a thing."

It came to her what was probably bothering him. "You don't trust her."

"No, that's not so. I think she was telling the absolute truth. I think Robert Atwood knows now that he doesn't have a prayer of taking Sam away from you, not under any circumstances."

Joleen realized she'd been holding her breath. She let it out in a rush. "Oh, Dekker. I believed her, too. But I couldn't completely allow myself to think that we were in the clear until I could hear it from you. I know, sometimes, I can be kind of a fool about trustin' people."

"You are no fool, Jo. And you're right about this. That woman's on the level. I'd stake my whole, newly acquired, totally unearned fortune on that."

So silly, but right then, she felt hesitant about going to him, putting her arms around him, laying her head against his heart. Why? "You know, you do seem kind of distant."

He shrugged again. "Just preoccupied. I should get over to the agency, check my messages. Who the hell knows what I've got there that I need to deal with."

Well, she was not allowing this strange feeling of distance that had popped up out of nowhere to get between them. She moved forward, wrapped her arms around his waist and put her head where she wanted it—against his broad chest. "I'd like to keep you here forever."

She felt his chuckle, a deep rumble against her ear. Was it just a little forced?

He kissed her, on the crown of her head, a sweet, warm pressure, his lips against her hair. And then he was taking her by the arms, setting her back from him. "Gotta go."

"But I—" She stopped herself from begging him to stay a few minutes longer. For heaven's sake, the man did have a business to run. He'd been totally hers for over a week now. And she was spoiled. Now they were back home, she was going to have to get used to giving him a little space.

She thought of Stacey and almost shivered, though the heater had done its job and the house was now cozy and warm. She was not going to become the kind of wife that Stacey had been—clinging and needful, never letting him have a moment to himself.

She put on a bright smile. "Well, go on, then. You get to work."

He turned from her. She trailed after him and stood there in the open doorway, the chilly air outside bringing up the goose bumps along her arms, watching as he hurried away from her down her front steps.

He called sometime later. She wasn't sure exactly when. She and Sam were out picking up a few groceries at the time. He left a message saying he had even more to deal with at the agency than he'd anticipated. He wouldn't be making it back for dinner at Camilla's. He didn't know when he'd get in.

And she shouldn't wait up for him.

She could hear it in his voice. Something *was* bothering him, in spite of his earlier denials.

She tried to call him. At the agency, and on his mobile phone. She got voice mail both places. She tried his apartment. Same thing.

Well, fine, she told herself as she put away the wedding gifts Camilla had left in the guest room for her while they were gone. He had to come home eventually. And she *would* insist they talk about it as soon as he did. However late it ended up being, she would be waiting up.

* * *

Right after dinner Camilla asked Niki to take Sam upstairs and keep an eye on him for a little while. "And you," she said to Joleen. "You come on with me."

"Mama…"

"Don't you 'mama' me. Come on. This way." Camilla grabbed Joleen's hand and dragged her toward the study, shutting the door behind them once they were inside.

Camilla folded her arms across her middle. "You've had a frown between your brows all evenin'. And Dekker is missing. I can hardly keep up with all the changes around here lately. I want you to tell me. Just tell me straight-out. What has gone wrong now?"

Joleen spoke with measured calm. "Dekker is not missing. He has work to do. He's been away for two weeks and—"

Camilla waved a slender hand. "Don't give me that. There is somethin' wrong here. I can see it in those eyes of yours. And I do not like it. This afternoon I was feelin' so good, too. I actually thought all of your problems were solved."

"Mama—"

Camilla shook her head. "No. Wait. Let me say what I have to say."

"But—"

"I mean it. Let your mother talk."

Joleen let out a groan and dropped into one of the soft, old chairs. "Oh, go ahead. As if I ever could stop you."

Camilla narrowed her eyes and pursed up her mouth. "Don't get righteous on me now, not after the way you have lied to me."

"Mama—"

"Shh. You think I wasn't bound to get it all figured out? You think your mama is a fool, she can't add two and two and come up with four? You two, you and Dekker. I know what you did, schemin' together, deciding to marry to keep Robert Atwood from having any chance of stealing Sam. I had it figured out from the first, even though you lied right in my face and said it wasn't so. I knew. A mother knows. And by the time Tony came looking for me at the shop, I'd done a little deep thinkin' on the subject. And it had come to me that maybe you and Dekker were not such an impossible pair after all."

Joleen shifted in her chair. "Oh, now, what is that supposed to mean?"

"It means, I got to thinking how it was for you two. That maybe it wasn't a problem of there being no spark between you, but that over and over again life had got in the way of you findin' out what you were to each other—first, with your daddy dying, God rest his sweet, sweet soul."

Joleen leaned forward. "Daddy dying? What does that have to do with—"

"Joly honey, you got so responsible after Samuel passed. You had no time for the love that was waitin' for you. And then, along comes that poor, pretty, mixed-up Stacey, getting between you and Dekker, snatchin' him away from you before you even knew he was yours in the first place. And then she hurt him. Hurt him down to his very soul. And after Stacey, well, there was that foolish, handsome Atwood boy. And then that boy dumped you and you had Sam. And by that time both you and Dekker had convinced yourselves that you were immune to love.

"But you know what I told you, that morning after you announced to the family that you and Dekker were tying the knot. It was the truth, what I told you. There is no mistake so big that love can't find a way to make it right in the end.

"Once I saw the truth about the two of you, I knew what you needed. A little time, in close quarters, away from it all. And that is why I didn't let Tony call you with the news that the custody battle was off. I wanted the two of you to have that time. I wanted you to have the chance to find out that you are not immune to love, that you love each other, in a soul deep, man and woman way."

Camilla parked her hands on her hips and let out a hard huff of breath. "And it worked, didn't it?" She waved a hand again. "You don't even have to answer. I saw you two together today. And there it was, at last. The fire, as well as the tenderness. You two have it all—or, at least, I could have sworn you did this afternoon."

Camilla fell silent. The beloved, shabby room seemed to echo with everything she had said.

Joleen swallowed the lump that had formed in her throat. And then she jumped from the chair.

"Oh, Mama…"

"Come here, baby. Here to me…" Her mother's arms were waiting. They closed around her.

"Oh, Mama. You are so right…"

"Well, of course I am, baby."

"But…something *is* wrong. I don't know what. He got so far away, all of a sudden, right after you and Antonia left this afternoon."

"You have told him, haven't you? You did say the words?"

"The words?"

Camilla took Joleen's face in her hands. "Honey, I mean, have you told him that you love him—as a *man?* Have you done that?"

Joleen swallowed again.

And her mother dropped her hands, stepped back and sent a look of pure exasperation heavenward. "Oh, well, I should have known. You haven't even *told* him."

"But, Mama, you don't know how it has been. We've been so happy, just livin' every minute for all it was worth. I didn't even think about telling him, about sitting him down and saying, 'Look, I love you. You are the only man for me.' It didn't even seem necessary to say it in words. Everything was going so wonderfully. It's been so beautiful. So right."

"It is necessary," her mother said softly. "He needs to hear that you love him, and he needs to hear it from your mouth."

"Yes. Yes, of course. I can see that. I can see that now."

"Tell him."

"I will."

"As soon as he has sense enough to come home to you."

"I promise."

"And then find out what happened this afternoon that made him pull away."

"Oh, Mama. I...I worry—"

"That is not news, baby. Since your daddy died, you have worried way too much."

"I mean, I worry that he'll think I'm like Stacey, clinging to him, making *demands* on him that he can't handle."

Camilla took her by the shoulders then and gave her a shake. "You listen. You listen to me. You are not Stacey. You never were and you never could be. You are a strong and self-sufficient woman who knows what she wants out of life, not to mention how to go about gettin' it. And Dekker knows that about you. He probably knows it even better than you do. Never, ever is he going to confuse you with that poor, troubled girl. Do you understand?"

"Yes, Mama. I do."

"Talk to him. Stick with him. Get *him* to talk to *you.*"

Chapter Seventeen

Dekker surprised her.

In spite of that message he'd left, saying he would be in late, he was waiting on her front porch, one leg slung up on the railing, when she got home from her mother's. A quick shaft of pure gladness passed through her at the sight of him, hunched down in his leather bomber jacket against the bite of the chilly night wind. And then apprehension rose up, tightening her stomach, making her heart beat a little faster than before.

He had his own key. She had given him one a year ago, when she first moved in. It bothered her—a lot—that he hadn't used it. It seemed as if he made a sort of statement, by not letting himself in, by waiting out here in the cold and the dark like a stranger, like someone who didn't have the right to enter her house when she wasn't home.

When he saw her drive up, he jumped down from the porch and jogged over to pull open the garage door for her. She drove her car in, got out and went to get Sam from the back seat.

Dekker waited for her to emerge and then lowered the door. She turned for the back steps, carrying her sleeping son on one shoulder.

When Dekker fell in beside her, she asked, carefully, "Why didn't you let yourself in? No need to sit out here in the cold."

He didn't answer. His silence, to her, seemed ominous. She sent him a glance. And for that she got a shrug that might have meant anything.

They went up the back steps. "I'll just put Sammy down," she said once they were inside.

"Fine."

She left him, turning the light on as she went out of the room.

She took Sammy to the bathroom and got him to use the toilet. Then she put him to bed, taking off his little jacket and his shoes and socks, but leaving him in his clothes so as not to wake him any more than she had already.

Once she'd tucked him beneath the covers, she kissed him, on his soft little cheek, taking comfort from the contact. Then she smoothed his hair off his forehead, whispered a good-night he did not hear and tiptoed from the room.

Dekker was waiting for her at the kitchen table. He had not helped himself to a beer, had not even taken off his jacket.

They looked at each other for a long, bleak moment. There were maybe four feet between them. But the look in his eyes told her it might as well have been a thousand miles.

Where have you been? she was thinking. What's the matter? What has gone wrong? The questions echoed in her head, but somehow not a one of them made its way out her mouth.

He was the one who spoke first. "I have a few things to say. A little...explaining to do."

She had to cough before she could get words out. "I...um, all right."

He tipped his head at the chair across from him. "Will you sit down?"

She slid into the chair, folded her hands on the tabletop.

"Well," he said, and cleared his throat.

She licked her lips, tightened her folded hands. She longed to tell him what was in her heart. But he had asked to go first. And she would give him that.

"Damn," he muttered. "Where the hell to begin..."

"Just—"

"What?"

Her mouth felt parched. She had to force the words through all that dryness. "Go ahead. It doesn't matter...where you start."

"How about this afternoon?" His voice was hard, heavy with sarcasm. "How about that? How about Antonia Atwood, showing up here, proving that all you had to do was wait a little, and there would have been no threat to Sammy."

She didn't quite see what he was getting at. "All right," she murmured. "What about Antonia? What about this afternoon."

He made a low noise, one of pure impatience. "Oh, come on. You know what. This afternoon proved that we never needed to get married in the first place. And we wouldn't have. If I hadn't pushed you into it, it never would have happened. You would have had to get through a nerve-racking week or so. And then Antonia would have stood up to that husband of hers and everything would have worked out all by itself. But I couldn't leave it, couldn't let the problem take care of itself. I had to…turn your life upside down. And for what? It's a very good question, don't you think?"

She still didn't know where he was leading her. But she could see very clearly that wherever—*whatever* it was—he was blaming himself.

"Dekker, you had no way of knowin' what Antonia would do. And you did not *push* me into our marriage. I was willing, more than willing. We both know that I was."

"Sure you were. Why wouldn't you be? We've been…such good friends. So…close."

"Why do you say it like that? Like there's something wrong with what we have been to each other? There is nothing wrong with you and me, together. Our friendship has been one of the best and most important things in my life."

"You trust me."

"I do. Absolutely. With my life. You know that."

"Well, yes I do know that. And I have to tell you, I lied in that message I left for you this afternoon."

"You lied…"

"That's right. I haven't really been at the agency. I've been at my apartment. Sitting. And thinking. All afternoon. Into the evening…"

"Thinking about what?"

He looked at her, a hard, unhappy look. And then, abruptly, he stood. "Look. What's the point of this? We don't really need to go into all the gory details."

"Yes, we—"

"No. We don't. The deal is, you don't need to be married to me anymore. The deal is, you never did."

She stared up at him, her heart feeling as if it was just shriveling down to nothing inside her chest. "What are you telling me, Dekker?"

"I am telling you that I'm going to give you that divorce we talked about at the first. The divorce we agreed we would get when Robert Atwood was no longer a threat to you. I'm telling you that I'm setting you free. Right away."

"But Dekker. I don't want to be free."

He stared at her with something that looked almost like pity. "Jo. You just don't get it. You don't even know...what you are. The kind of woman you are. The kind of man you deserve. Who have you been with? That idiot, Atwood. And me. You can do better. You *will* do better."

She could not stay in that chair. She leaped to her feet. "I keep trying, trying to say it, to tell you how I really feel. I think I am sending out a very clear message. But somehow, you are not receiving. I will say it slowly. And I will say it clearly. Dekker, there is no one—*no one*—who is better than you."

He only shook his head.

She felt as if she was slipping down a hill, grabbing at rocks and bushes, trying her hardest to halt the fall. And not succeeding. So she blurted it out. "Dekker, I love you. I love you with all of my heart. You are my husband. And I'm glad, so glad that you are. I don't care how we got to it, what little lies we had to tell each other to give ourselves permission to take the big step. We're married. I want us to stay that way. I love you and I don't want anyone else.''

For half of an instant she thought she had him. Something like hope flared in those deep-blue eyes. But then hope faded. His eyes went flat. He spoke low. ''You say that because it's not in you to say anything else. You are loyal to a fault.''

''Dekker, I say it because it is the truth!''

''Don't you get what I'm telling you? This whole thing, you and me, our wild time in Baja, I think…I wanted that. I think I wanted it bad. I think I've wanted it for a long time now, with you, and I've been looking for a way to give myself permission to have it.''

''So? What's wrong with that?''

''I told you. You can do better. Damn it, I *love* you. I want the best for you.''

''You love me.'' Her shriveled heart expanded to hard-beating life again. ''You said it. You heard yourself. You admitted that you love me.''

''That is not the point.''

''Oh, yes. It is. It is exactly the point.'' She started for him.

He threw up a warding-off hand. ''Stay there. Don't come any closer. I want you to have the best life can give you. And I am not it.''

She stayed where she was—but she spoke with the absolute conviction of the love that she bore him. ''Oh, yes you are. There is no one better, truer, more *right* for me than you.''

He looked at her as if she had lost her mind. "What are you talking about? Look at my damn life. I mean, who the hell am I, anyway? I can't help but wonder— and you should wonder, too. My 'mother,' in reality, was my kidnapper. In a way, my whole life has been a lie. I married a woman with serious emotional problems. And then, when things got tough, I turned my back on her. She committed suicide. And I almost gave up completely. I left the department, just walked away, kissed all my ambitions and dreams goodbye. I would probably be dead myself now, if not for you. I run a two-bit detective agency over a coin laundry in a badly maintained building downtown. And a few weeks ago I found out who my real family is, I found out I happen to be a very rich man. But that's all I've got going for me, and that just dropped into my damn lap. I am a—"

That was it. All she could take. She cleared the two feet that stood between them and clapped her hand over his mouth. "You shut up, Dekker Sm—" she caught herself "—Dekker Bravo. I will not hear such things from you, such lies, such a terrible, cruel twisting of the truth. I am sorry, so sorry, about Stacey. About the hell she lived in, in her own mind. And the hell we both know she put you through. You could not have saved her. Nobody could have saved her— except Stacey herself. And she...well, she did not manage it. And that did almost kill you. Because you loved her. And you *hurt* for her, for all she was, for all she could have been, for all she could not get past.

"But what happened to Stacey was not your fault. And you only hurt yourself more, hurt everyone who loves you, by not letting her go, not forgiving yourself and getting on with your life.''

He grabbed her then, grabbed her by the arms and hauled her up against him. His eyes burned into hers. "You can say that. You can say that, because—"

"Because it is true," she said right into his face, pressing herself closer, harder, tighter to him than he was already holding her. "Because I love you, I love you with all I have got in me to love. I love you as my dearest, closest friend. As my husband, the one I want to share my life with. And as the lover who sets my body on fire."

"Don't," he said, the word desperate, low, very rough. His hands hurt her, his fingers were like bands of steel on her arms.

And she didn't care, she could take the pain. All she cared about was that he never, under any circumstances, let her go.

"Don't?" She handed the word right back to him. "Don't what? Don't tell you the truth? Don't ask you to stop lying, putting yourself down, trying to turn away from me and calling it for my own good? What are you saying, you are not good enough? Who has been the man in my family for ten years? Who shows up to fix the faucet when it won't stop leaking? Who bails my crazy sisters out of jail? Who shows my little boy, by example, every day, what it is to be a man, to be the one we all can count on?''

"Jo, I—"

"Nope. Not. Wait. Oh, you have made me good and mad, Dekker Bravo. And as for your life being a lie, well, maybe Lorraine did keep a terrible secret from you. But everyone knows how much that woman loved you. She loved you more than her own life. And what about us, huh, what about all us Tillys and DuFraynes? What you have, with the family, well, that is no lie. You had a pretty good childhood, all in all. And I think I ought to know, bein' as how I was there.''

"Jo…''

She realized she was crying. Crying. She couldn't believe it. She *never* cried. The tears dribbled down her cheeks. She would have swiped the damn things away with a vengeance if he hadn't had such a tight grip on her arms.

"And besides.'' She had to pause to sniff good and hard. "Besides, poor Lorraine is like Stacey. She's gone from us now. Time to forgive her. Time to move on. The sins of the past have been set right, I would say, as much as they ever can be.''

He said her name, again, in a whisper this time. And then he released his cruel grip on her arms. He cupped her face, hands gone suddenly so very tender, and rubbed at her tears with his thumbs. "Damn it…''

Oh, he was losing it. She could see it in those beautiful blue-black eyes. He was wanting her, she could feel that as she pressed herself so close against his body. He was…giving in, though he kept fighting it, giving in to love…

She stretched that little bit closer, just close enough to brush her lips against his. His breath caught.

She whispered against his mouth, "What are you talking about? Who do you think you are kidding? I deserve better, you say? Better than you? So what will that mean, then, if you do let me go? If we get that divorce and I start in with other men, trying to find with another what I've already got with you? Are you going to stand still for that, for some other guy putting his hands on me? Is that what you're telling me, you're going to sit by and watch me get *what I deserve* with some other man?''

He swore again, this time a word that burned her ears when she heard it.

She kept right after him, utterly shameless, pressing her breasts up to his chest, her hips to his thighs, letting the tears stream, unheeded down her cheeks. ''Tell me, Dekker. Try to tell me that lie....''

That did it. His control broke. He took her mouth, hard. With a glad, triumphant cry, she parted her lips and sucked his tongue inside.

He wrapped his arms around her so tight, it knocked the breath from her body. Then he started walking her backward, across her kitchen floor. He turned into her bedroom, shoved the door shut with his heel.

His hands were all over her. And she gloried in every hungry, grasping touch. They tore at each other's clothes, not bothering to take them off completely, only what they had to get rid of to get to each other.

He unhooked her bra, yanked her shirt up, latched that hot mouth of his onto her breast. She left him his jacket and his shirt, but went right to work unbuttoning his jeans, shoving them and his boxers down enough to free him.

The flared slacks she wore were something else again. They had to come all the way down and off, along with her panties.

She felt the air against the flesh of her legs. She was

naked from waist to ankles, though her shoes and socks were still on.

He lifted her. She went with a glad cry, wrapping her legs around him, sliding her wetness down onto him, taking him inside.

He groaned. She took his mouth, took that groan into herself. He surged upward, filling her.

She stilled, opened her eyes, saw *his* eyes gleaming at her through the gloom of her dark bedroom. "Say it," she commanded. "Say you love me. Say it now."

He swore again.

She did not waver. "Say it."

He groaned again. And he gave her what she wanted. "I love you." He swore once more. "Love you, love you, love you, Jo…"

"Say you'll stay with me. Never leave me. Be my husband. Forever. As long we both have breath in our bodies, you will be mine and I will be yours."

"Jo…" He pressed up into her.

She shook her head, refusing to move with him. "I know it. I know it already. You are mine and you are not going to leave me. Because I know you. You wouldn't…do this, with me, now. Under no circumstances, but most especially not like this, without any protection. You wouldn't. Unless you had completely surrendered. Unless you finally understood exactly where you belong."

"You are killing me…"

"No. I am loving you. And I…I want you to—I *beg* you to—say it." He shifted beneath her, just the tiniest bit. "No! Don't you move. Not until you say it."

He made a guttural sound, something dragged up from the depths of him.

Tenderly she put her hand across his mouth. "Oh, say it. Please, please say it…"

He moaned.

"Yes. You can. You can say it to me…."

"I will…never leave you. I will…be your husband…"

"Forever."

"Forever. As long as we both have breath in our bodies…I am yours, Jo. Always. I am yours…."

"Oh," she said. "Oh, yes…that's it. That is exactly it."

He pushed into her, hard.

"Yes! Oh, Dekker, yes…"

And the rest was pure magic. Hard and frantic. Wild and wet and fine.

When at last he slumped, spent, against the door, she whispered her love tenderly. He whispered his back to her.

He staggered to the bed with her and carefully laid her down.

They were naked in no time. He came into her waiting arms. She pulled the covers over them. They lay awake for another hour or two, whispering softly, sharing secrets and plans.

And then, wrapped up close and warm, together in the truest sense—man and wife, passionate lovers, the very best of friends—they drifted off to sleep.

They bought a seven-bedroom house, right next to Mesta Park in Heritage Hills. It was a beautiful old place with lots of interesting woodwork and lustrous hardwood floors, high ceilings and crown moldings and fine beveled glass in the windows.

The yard was a good size, had a pool and a brick fence around the perimeter, with an iron gate across the wide driveway. The fence and the gate went a long way toward discouraging the prying eyes of the press. And anyone the fence and gate didn't take care of, Dekker's pricey security system did.

In April, they threw a big party, for family near and far. It was a housewarming and also an opportunity to renew their wedding vows.

Bravos came from all over—Emma, Jonas and Mandy from Los Angeles, of course. And Marsh Bravo—Dekker and Jonas's cousin—and Marsh's family, too. They lived in Norman, just a twenty-minute drive from Oklahoma City. Marsh was the evil Blake's son, the one who had found the first clues to the terrible deed his father had done. And there were more. Some second cousins, from Florida and from Northern California—a pair of sisters, with their husbands and children. And from Wyoming, three other second cousins, and their wives and sons and daughters, as well.

There were a lot of Tillys, of course. And all the usual DuFraynes. And Antonia and Robert Atwood. Antonia positively glowed, and Robert stayed close to her, clearly smitten in spite of himself with his newly confident wife.

After a particularly gruesome binge around Christmastime, Uncle Hubert had joined Alcoholics Anonymous. He was sticking with it, too, attending meetings regularly, drinking only ginger ale at social occasions. So Joleen didn't have to worry about taking care of him as the party progressed.

But there were plenty of other crises to deal with. Niki had found her first boyfriend. They were having some kind of fight. Niki kept bursting into tears at regular intervals. And DeDe was pregnant. She had trouble holding her food down, threw up on the back patio and then ran, mortified and sobbing, into the house. She locked herself in the upstairs bathroom and it took both Wayne and Joleen to coax her out.

Then there was Mama, who had a new boyfriend with whom she flirted and carried on in a shameless fashion. This was the third or fourth since the ice cream man back in October. They just never lasted. But Camilla claimed she was happy. And Joleen had to admit that she did seem to be, especially now that she and Antonia were so close. The boyfriends might come and go, but when Camilla Tilly found a true woman friend, it was always for life.

Dekker and Joleen renewed their vows after darkness fell, by the golden light of several rows of pretty paper lanterns strung from tree to tree, under the steady silver glow of a glorious full moon.

And as Dekker Bravo promised anew to love, honor and cherish Joleen for the rest of their lives, it came to him that the past truly had been put to rest. When he looked into his wife's loving eyes, all doubt was vanquished. He knew exactly who he was.

The stolen Bravo Baby had found his way home at last.

* * * * *

Beloved author
Sherryl Woods
is back with a brand-new miniseries

THE CALAMITY JANES

Five women. Five Dreams.
A lifetime of friendship....

On Sale May 2001—DO YOU TAKE THIS REBEL?
Silhouette Special Edition

On Sale August 2001—COURTING THE ENEMY
Silhouette Special Edition

On Sale September 2001—TO CATCH A THIEF
Silhouette Special Edition

On Sale October 2001—THE CALAMITY JANES
Silhouette Single Title

On Sale November 2001—WRANGLING THE REDHEAD
Silhouette Special Edition

"Sherryl Woods is an author who writes with
a very special warmth, wit, charm and intelligence."
—*New York Times* bestselling author
Heather Graham Pozzessere

Available at your favorite retail outlet.

Where love comes alive™

Visit Silhouette at www.eHarlequin.com   SSETCJR

Celebrate the season with

Midnight Clear

A holiday anthology featuring
a classic Christmas story from
New York Times bestselling author

Debbie Macomber

Plus a brand-new *Morgan's Mercenaries* story
from *USA Today* bestselling author

Lindsay McKenna

And a brand-new *Twins on the Doorstep* story
from national bestselling author

Stella Bagwell

Available at your favorite retail outlets in November 2001!

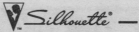

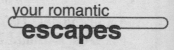

Silhouette Books cordially invites you to come
on down to Jacobsville, Texas, for

DIANA PALMER's
LONG, TALL TEXAN
Weddings

(On sale November 2001)

The LONG, TALL TEXANS series from international
bestselling author Diana Palmer is cherished around the
world. Now three sensuous, charming love stories from
this blockbuster series—*Coltrain's Proposal, Beloved* and
"Paper Husband"—are available in one special volume!

*As free as wild mustangs, Jeb, Simon and Hank vowed
never to submit to the reins of marriage. Until, of course,
a certain trio of provocative beauties tempt these Lone Star
lovers off the range…and into a tender, timeless embrace!*

**You won't want to miss
LONG, TALL TEXAN WEDDINGS
by Diana Palmer, featuring two
full-length novels and one short story!**

Available only from Silhouette Books at your favorite retail outlet.

Where love comes alive™